I0519552

Bobbin' For One Bad Apple

A Willow Crier Cozy Mystery

Book 5

Lilly York

Bobbin' For One Bad Apple

A Willow Crier Cozy Mystery

Book 5

©2016 by Lilly York

www.lillyyork.com

Cover Design: Jonna Feavel
40daygraphics.com

Illustrations: Ben Gerhards

Interior Layout: Daniel Mawhinney
40daypublishing.com

Published by: Wide Awake Books
wideawakebooks.com

Also available in eBook publication

Printed in the United States of America

Get your FREE short story

Grandpa Goes Missing

Find out what happened to bring Willow down to Oklahoma in the first place.

Be the first in line to read Lilly York's latest books, get extra recipes from Willow's kitchen, get 'sneak peeks' on works-in-progress, receive special offers and so much more…

FREE short story only available here! Get yours today.

https://lillyyork.com/shortstory

Also by Lilly York

The Willow Crier Cozy Mystery Series

Chili to Die For (Book 1)

I Scream, You Scream (Book 2)

This Little Piggy Wound Up Dead (Book 3)

Southern Fried Son of a Gun (Book 4)

Bobbin' for One Bad Apple (Book 5)

Chocolate Kiss of Death (Book 6)

The Brother Bay Cozy Mystery Series

In-Laws & Out-Laws (Book 1)

Catch & Release (Book 2)

Chapter 1

Willow walked in a slow circle. Everything in her ice cream shop had taken on the appearance of fall. Various shades of red, yellow, orange, and brown were scattered everywhere. Turtle's fall festival was celebrated in conjunction with Halloween and Willow wanted to be sure her store was decorated to the hilt. She glanced out the front windows and her spirit sulked. The grass, the trees, all of nature had dressed in drab gray. No autumn colors to be seen. If she couldn't have the real thing—fall in the north where fall really happened—she'd improvise. She had trees with fall leaves, pumpkins, gourds, bales of hay, even a scarecrow. She wanted to have bobbing for apples, but Molly talked her into having a maze in the small open lot behind the ice cream store as her attraction, thereby giving Molly the apple bobbing attraction.

She was looking forward to the celebration. In a few hours, children dressed as ghosts and goblins would be visiting her shop for complimentary apple donuts and spiced apple cider. Of course, she would have other apple and pumpkin goodies for sale too, like her German apple cake and her grandmother's apple pie, as well as scrumptious pumpkin bars. A personal favorite. Her mouth watered just thinking about her favorite fall treats.

The door opened and Willow's face fell. The jogging complainers, as she liked to call them, came calling. She stood behind the counter and waited for the barrage of instructions. As well as the complaints.

He, being the gentleman that he was, ordered first. "I'll have a low-fat milk latte, 2 shots of espresso, no foam, extra hot, with three packets of Splenda stirred in well." No hello. No please. No thank you.

Willow looked to his wife, at least Willow thought she was his wife. The petite dark-haired beauty said, "I'm lactose intolerant, so I'll have the same except make mine with soy milk, oh, and Splenda seems to upset my tummy so use Agave nectar."

Willow tried very hard not to roll her eyes. "We still do not have Agave nectar. I'm sorry." She gave her the same story as she did the day before, and the day before that—when she made a run to the city she'd swing by Whole Foods, until then, she'd have to use one of the sweeteners she had on hand.

"Uh, sheesh, I miss home. You can't get a decent cup of coffee in this town." She told her husband who was looking at his watch for the tenth time. "Fine. Use Splenda. I'll suffer."

Willow couldn't help but overhear the young woman whisper, "Do you have an appointment or something?"

He gave her a dirty look and she promptly clamped her lips together.

Willow got the conversation back on track. "You could use sugar."

The gasp coming from both joggers was loud enough to be heard in the far corner of the ice cream side of her shop. Willow's eyes widened. Their gasps caused her concern.

"Sugar? You must be joking. Haven't touched the stuff in years. It's poison." Her face pinched, as if she were in pain, when she glanced at the treats behind the glass counter. "You really shouldn't sell that stuff. Doing so is irresponsible and advocating bad eating habits."

"Karla, don't distract her. You know these people can barely do one thing at a time, let alone multitask." He smiled a tight-lipped grin in Willow's direction then he lowered his voice. "She'll probably mess the coffee up as it is."

Karla laughed. "Good one, Flynn."

Willow mimicked their New York accent to a tee as she turned around to grab the soy milk. "Did you hear that Janie? Can't get a decent cup of cawhfee in dis town."

Janie was making shakes for a group of teenage girls. "Shh, they'll hear you."

"I don't give a rip. Rude, arrogant, stuck up…"

Janie placed her hand over Willow's mouth. "Be nice. Don't lower yourself to their level. We've got to keep our spirits up. The kids will be coming soon."

Willow licked the chocolate that had transferred from Janie's hand. "Mm, that's good. I might have to have one of those later."

Willow made their drinks with an attitude, not that they noticed. She doubted they considered anyone besides themselves. She handed them the drinks, collected the money, and sent them on their way. Of course, they didn't leave a tip. Willow didn't expect anything more from the matching twins from up yonder. The sooner she had them out of her hair, the sooner she could manage an attitude adjustment and finish prepping for the kids. She glanced at her watch.

"Janie, I'm going to go check and see how Embry and Marshall are doing on the maze then

I'm going to walk to the café and see how Molly is doing. I'll be back in a bit."

Everyone was hands on, including the part-timers, for the event so she wasn't concerned about leaving Janie shorthanded. The maze was awesome. Willow spent a good ten minutes laughing her way through it. Embry and Marshall each had a chair, one at the beginning and one at the end of the maze and walkie talkies to keep in touch. How many in, how many out. Marshall was sitting at the exit with the big bowl of candy. He said he'd sacrifice himself. Embry had the entry. No candy for her. She was trying to lose weight before the wedding. Willow thought she was perfect just as she was but all brides wanted to look their best, Embry was no exception.

After successfully navigating the maze, Willow meandered down to the café where Molly had made a giant batch of caramel to go with the apples the kids would be bobbing for. A little something sweet to dip the apples in. It was a holiday, after all. Willow was looking forward to sampling the sweet treat she'd heard Molly talking about. *Maybe she'll let me bob for the first apple*. Willow reminisced about fall trips to the apple orchard. She sighed. The apples were so good, so crisp, she'd usually made several trips during the season.

She made a sound of disgust as she walked through the front door to see Flynn and Karla arguing with poor Molly. She heard Molly's reply to whatever they had been complaining about.

"This isn't New York or California. This is Oklahoma. We do things a bit different. At this time of year, we actually give our kids candy." She gave Karla a look that Willow had a hard time interpreting.

Karla stuck her nose up in the air and walked out. Flynn was right behind her.

Willow held the door open for them as they flew by her without so much as a thank you, then she wiped her hands together, as if there was dirt on them and she had to get it off. "I see you've tossed out the rubbish."

"If only. He thinks the sun comes up just to hear him crow. And she's no better. You can take the girl out of the country but you can't take the country out of the girl."

Willow stared, dumbfounded. "What on earth are you talking about, Molly?"

"Ain't it obvious? The man thinks he's the authority on all things. He won't shut up."

"No, I got that. I'm talking about Karla. What did you mean?"

"Oh, I forget you're not from around these parts. Karla's about as southern as a girl can get. She was born and raised an Okie. Then off she went up north to college and she decided we're not sophisticated enough for her, so she migrated, like them birds that go north for summer. Claims she was born in the wrong skin."

"You have to be kidding me?"

"Nope. Her daddy and mama live on the ranch next to mine. You'd never know it but growing up that girl was at my house more than she was her own." Molly shook her head. "My niece has broken my sister's heart."

Willow's mouth dropped. *Niece?* She swallowed hard and remained silent.

Molly continued. "This is the first time she's been home since she left for college. Hardly ever calls her mama. Miriam's learned the hard way she's got to trust God with Karla. Otherwise she'd be a worryin' mess."

Willow headed back to her own shop. She waved to Steve and his deputy who were letting kids sit in the front seat of the police car and passing out candy to everyone who passed. All evening, in between the princesses and knights, Willow thought about the rude couple from New York. How could that girl be an Okie? And Molly's niece? She certainly didn't treat her like one would treat an aunt. Since moving from Wisconsin, she complained about the heat, the bugs, the snakes, her allergies, and the tornadoes. But never the people. The friendliest people on earth. She'd swear by it. What in the world happened to that girl?

The next morning, Willow woke to the sound of her chirping cell phone. "Darn. Why didn't I turn off the ringer?" She picked it up and muttered, "This better be good."

Janie responded. "Get down to Molly's, now. Flynn went bobbing for apples and he never came up.

Chapter 2

Willow dressed in discarded clothes from the night before and ran out the door. She popped a mint in her mouth as she drove. Poor Clover, she hurried her to do her business then put her in the laundry room. Her new habit was taking nasty used tissues out of the garbage and chewing them up. She was on lock up—again! Darn dog got herself into the most trouble!

The sidewalk in front of Molly's was cordoned off and the door was locked so Willow knocked on the glass. Steve looked up from his position next to the body and waved her in. One of his deputies unlocked the door, warning her not to touch anything.

Her facial expression let him know she wasn't a novice. She thought it odd that Flynn looked the same in death as he did in life. Not a hair was out of place. His angular, sometimes bony, facial features still were aristocratic. His jet-black hair still sported the $200 haircut and his perfectly manicured hands looked better than Willow's.

"What happened?"

Steve stood up. "Take a look for yourself." He held out his hand and gave her the freedom to examine the scene and body.

Flynn, wearing the same clothes he'd been in last night, was on his knees, hands limp next to his legs, head in the water turned slightly, his profile clearly showing, with apples bobbing all around him. There were no visible bruises on his neck, nothing that would indicate he'd been held down under the water. "How weird. I mean, who willingly puts their head in water and drowns themselves?

She saw something glitter in the water, the deputy had been blocking the eastern light and when he moved, something sparkled. "Steve," she pointed to the water. "Look. Something besides apples is in the water."

"Um, Willow, it's Flynn's head."

She rolled her eyes. "Come here." She pointed again. "See? It's right there." She turned to look at Steve who was still looking confused. When she turned to the water, she noticed the deputy was once again blocking the sun light. She walked to him, physically moved him and told him to stay there.

"Now, look again."

"Huh, look at that. We would have found it when we emptied the tub but, good eye." He put on long gloves and pulled out a gorgeous diamond ring. "Wow. They don't get much bigger than that." He motioned for an evidence bag then deposited the ring for safe keeping. "This gives us a place to start." He asked the deputy to pick up Karla and take her to the station for questioning.

It was no secret among the locals that Flynn was not welcome in most of the shops…or the homes. He was an ungrateful, arrogant northerner who didn't have a lick of kindness in him. But that didn't mean anyone disliked him enough to kill him. And this definitely smelled like murder.

Willow looked around the crime scene a little longer but nothing else popped. Molly was quietly crying in a booth in the back of the café. Willow poured them both a cup of coffee and sat down across from her. As the medical examiner took the body and more evidence was collected, Steve joined them.

He patted her hand. "What happened?"

She trembled. "I don't know. I came in the back door this morning and did my usual prep work. I didn't even come out to the dining room. I knew I had a few things to clean up but I needed to get the breakfast basics going first. By the time I finished up back there, turned on the lights for the dining room, it was after five." She started crying all over again. "To think I'd been working back there with a dead body in my dining room for over an hour."

Millie pulled out a tissue from her purse and Steve removed a handkerchief from his pocket at the same time. Molly took both. She would need them.

"Janie called me. How did she find out?"

"I let my part-timer in before I noticed the body. We both noticed at the same time and she took off running and screaming. Janie must have seen her running in the street and stopped to ask me what was wrong. She called Steve then she called you." She wiped her nose. "Our crime scene professionals."

Willow raised her eyebrows in Steve's direction. He smirked. She didn't bother correcting Molly. Steve could handle being compared with an amateur. Especially when said amateur was as good at solving crimes as he was.

Willow asked, "Did Flynn and Karla come back in last night? After they stormed out of here?"

Steve asked in reply, "Stormed?"

"Wrong choice of words, obviously. They were upset because we were all giving the kids candy for the festival. Being a bad example, ruining their health, all that jazz, you know, you've heard it before. Molly was trying to explain and they got offended and went off in a huff. That's all. It happened in my store too. Not quite as up in arms about it, but they certainly let me know what they thought of all the treats in my case."

Molly interrupted. "That's not all it was about." She looked a bit panicked. "You didn't hear everything."

Willow and Steve sat quietly, waiting for her to wipe her eyes and nose and tell them the other part of the conversation.

"You see, when Karla left Turtle she was dating John New Moon." She paused. "Such a nice young man." Molly stared into space for a few seconds.

"Molly, go on."

"Oh, sorry. I was just remembering how the kids would all gather at our ranch and he had these big brown puppy dog eyes…he would just stare at her, like she was the only other person in the world."

Steve got her back on track. "Molly, what happened?"

"Oh, yeah, right. Well, John ended up doing real good. He's some kind of big wig in the oil business. Someone must have told him Karla was back in town and he showed up at her parent's ranch. I know cause I was there visitin' my brother. There was a big ruckus. Flynn got mad and left. So did John. And so did Karla. They all left, separate, but at the same time. Everybody was mad. Karla's parents were none too happy about Flynn and when John came knockin' on the door, they let him right in. I'm not sayin' I agree with what they did, but I understand. Flynn was bad news." She looked over at the ME working on the now stretched out body and let out a sob. "They wanted someone better for their daughter. I wanted someone better for my niece." She rested her head on her arms and sobbed.

Willow felt sorry for the sweet woman who welcomed her into the fold when she'd first taken over the ice cream shop. She was a pleasant woman, on the short side, a little plump, but in all the right places, and her soft heart always looked for someone to shower kindness upon. She and Willow had become fast friends.

Steve and Willow excused themselves from the booth then carried on their conversation quietly on the other side of the restaurant. Willow felt the electricity between them whenever they were near. He still gave her goosebumps.

"We need to speak with both Karla and John."

"Steve, I didn't see that ring on Karla's finger yesterday. I have no idea who that belongs to. Unless she was hiding it from everyone and only wearing it in private...that would mean things weren't all that good between them."

Steve pondered the thought. "Which would also mean she was here too, with Flynn."

Willow added, "And if that ring is hers, well, did she get mad at him, throw the ring, then kill him? That's pretty extreme. I've heard of some rough breakups, but there really didn't seem to be anything wrong between the two of them yesterday. In fact, they were both equally as irritating." She shook her head. "This theory doesn't make sense."

"Well, maybe John re-entered the picture and Karla remembered what she lost. If the rumors are true, Flynn wasn't exactly a gentleman."

"No, that he wasn't." Willow agreed.

"I'll never understand how a girl who was raised as the light in her daddy's eyes could settle for a man who treated her like she was a second-class citizen."

Willow understood. She had been introduced to southern gentlemen after moving to Oklahoma. Her grandfather was one, but she was around him more as a child and didn't notice how different his behavior was from a lot of other men she was around. Now that she was living in the south, and dating one of those southern gentlemen, she understood fully what Steve was referring to. It took some getting used to, that was for sure. But, now? She never wanted to be treated otherwise.

She took his hand and squeezed it. "A southern gentleman should never be taken for granted."

He smiled back. "I'm surprised Janie didn't have to go roll you out of bed."

"When my friends need me, I can get up."

He kissed her cheek. "I know, I'm just teasin'. Want to go talk to Karla with me?"

Chapter 3

Willow made sure someone was with Molly before going to the station with Steve. Seeing the boyfriend of your niece murdered in your place of business could not be easy. With the body removed from the restaurant, she seemed to be settling down—a little bit. The tub of apples was also gone. The deputy was still dusting for finger prints and collecting anything that might be out of place, but being a restaurant, there could be hundreds if not thousands of prints. The only hope there would be if there were a set of prints out of place, like a wanted man in twenty different states—which was completely unlikely. Nonetheless, they had to try.

Steve led Willow into the station and poured her a cup of coffee.

She grimaced as she took a sip. "Too bad I'm desperate."

"You need to be alert. This thick liquid works like magic. It will wake you up a lot better than that frou frou coffee you serve at the coffee shop."

Her mouth dropped. "I haven't heard you complain about our coffee before." She looked around the burnt orange and brown outdated, run down office. The coffee was a perfect match.

"I'm not complaining now. I'm just saying there's a time for frou frou and a time for a heavy dose of caffeine that'll stick to your ribs and grow hair..." He took a drink of his own and nearly scowled. "Times like these require the latter." He took another sip and grinned sheepishly. "OK, you're right. It's bad. Yours is much better." He raised his eyebrows. "Want to go get us some?"

She laughed.

The deputy knocked on the open door. "Chief. Bad news. Karla didn't come home last night. We don't know where she is."

Steve nodded. "Put out an all alert. We need to find her." He added, "When you've finished doing that, give John New Moon a call, ask him to come down to the station. We need to talk with him too."

The deputy nodded then walked to his desk.

Willow swirled the thick black liquid in her Styrofoam cup. "You know these aren't good for the landfills, don't you?"

"We're buying mugs, we just need someone to wash them. You volunteering?"

"No, but since we don't have anyone to interview, want to go to the coffee shop with me? Who knows, maybe Janie saw something. And we can get a decent cup of coffee while we're there."

Steve rose. "You don't have to twist my arm. I'm game."

The coffee shop was in full swing. Willow had no idea how rumors spread that quickly, but in Turtle, Oklahoma, rumors seemed to travel telepathically. Everyone in the whole town knew almost immediately after something happened. Since the café was still closed, being the scene of the crime and all, the next best place to congregate and throw out possible scenarios and spread gossip, was Willow's coffee shop. She and Steve had to fight for a table—in her own shop.

Good thing she and Janie anticipated a busy morning, not this busy, but Janie had extra help. The day after a town do, like the fall festival, was usually busy. Something, not usually murder, always happened and whatever the happening was, it had to be discussed. Today's news blew everything else out of the water.

The muffins were pumpkin and cream cheese with a touch of cinnamon. Heaven. And the coffee was amazing. Especially after drinking the swill from the station.

"You're so lucky you're dating me." She grinned.

"I seem to remember police officers get free coffee here anyway."

She grinned. "But they don't get free muffins."

He took a large bite and muttered, "You're so right. Definitely glad I'm dating the boss."

All sorts of conversations were taking place around them.

"Karla had enough of that no good for nothing…and she dumped him, literally, in the apple bucket."

"Flynn and Karla are on the run from the mob. They run cities like New York. That's the only reason she came back."

"Did you hear Flynn was having an affair with that girl from the bookstore? I saw them together. They thought they were alone."

"Molly got sick of how he treated her niece and she killed him. It happened in her shop. It's the logical conclusion."

Steve gave Willow a sly grin and waited for the crowd to clear out. Thankfully most of them had got sick of gossiping and had to be at a job somewhere, or kids to get off to school, or grocery shop for the evening's dinner, or some such thing which gave them a good reason to get up and leave. When the coffee shop was nearly empty, both Willow and Steve noticed a woman in a hat and dark sunglasses sitting in a quiet corner. They looked at one another and spoke at the same time. "Karla!"

The young woman's face jerked up. She took off her glasses and the beginning of a nice shiner was evident. Steve and Willow joined her, with a carafe of fresh coffee and a muffin for the girl.

They pulled up chairs without being invited.

Karla's dark sunglasses covered nearly half her face. Her dark hair was pulled back through a baseball cap and she was dressed in a pair of jeans and a flannel shirt. This was the first time she actually looked like she belonged on a ranch in Oklahoma, even if her shirt was a little too big on her.

Steve started. "Are you OK? What happened?"

Not only did she have a black eye but her eyes were swollen from a prolonged cry. A good long one if Willow's estimates were accurate.

"No, I'm not OK. Flynn…Flynn…he…"

Willow took her hand. "I know. I know. It's going to be hard to go on without him."

Karla straightened up. "How do you know?"

Willow answered with a question. "How do I know that Flynn's dead?"

Karla screamed and fainted.

Steve scowled. "Nice going."

"What did I do? Don't tell me she was sitting here with all the talk going on around her and didn't know that everyone was talking about her…and her dead husband or boyfriend or fiancé…or whatever he was, is on a slab in the morgue! She had to have known."

They both looked at the slumped over young woman.

Steve shook his head. "Apparently not."

Both worked on reviving her. "Karla, wake up. Come on, wake up." Willow rubbed her hand and stroked her cheek. She found her feelings toward the girl softening. *Everyone looks innocent when they're sleeping.*

Karla started to groan and slowly opened her eyes. Her confusion quickly turned to panic. "Dead? Did you say dead?"

"I'm sorry, I really thought you knew." Willow felt horrible. What a way to find out the guy you love is dead.

[28]

She violently shook her head. "No, it can't be true."

Steve closed his eyes then slowly re-opened them. Willow could almost read his mind. *Two crying women in one day!*

Willow was much gentler this time, "Yes, I'm sorry, but he has passed away."

A still small voice asked, "How?"

Steve let Willow answer.

"Well, his body was found in Molly's Café this morning. He…" she paused, not quite knowing how to tell Karla how he was found "…had his head in the apple bucket. We're not sure what happened, but that is how he was found."

She gasped and looked at her bare ring finger.

Willow continued. "Karla, did something happen between you and Flynn last night?"

She nodded, the floodgates opening once again. "We broke up and I threw my ring in the water. He must have went searching for it after I stormed out. But, how could he have drowned? No one else was there and he was extremely healthy."

"We really don't know yet. Everything is being checked out. Why did you break up?"

"He…he…he…" She tried to speak but developed the hiccups and started over each time her voice jumped. "He was mad because John showed up. He thought I'd go back to John. He got really angry and well…"

"Did he hit you?"

She nodded. "He punched me in the eye so hard I ended up on the floor. He's pushed me around some, but he never punched me before. I got mad and threw his ring. It landed in the water. I ran out the door and he, well, he must have tried to find the ring. That ring seemed to be more important to him than I ever was. He was always throwing it up in my face."

For the first time Steve entered the questioning. "How did you get in the café?"

"We picked the kitchen lock. This building has been around since I was a kid. We would hang out in here after hours back when old man Scranton owned it. All the locals knew how to get in. We never did any harm. Just hung out. Sometimes we'd sneak a soda but we'd always leave a few bills on the counter to cover the cost. The old man knew about it and never said a word. As long as we were respectful about it, we were good."

"What about John New Moon?"

She lifted her face. "What about him?"

"Was he with you in the café last night?"

She paused slightly then shook her head. "No."

"Did you see him after you left the café?"

She shook her head again.

Steve studied her for a few seconds.

"Karla, until all this is straightened out, I don't want you leaving town, OK?" After she agreed he added, "Do you have John's phone number? I'd like to talk to him."

She looked at her phone and rattled off a number.

"Thanks. Do you need me to call someone to come and pick you up?"

"No, that's OK. My car is parked down the street."

After she left Steve said, "She had John's phone number awful handy. I wonder if she's telling us the truth about not seeing him yesterday evening."

Willow added. "And I wonder whose shirt she is wearing 'cause it's certainly not hers."

Chapter 4

Willow stood on the service side of the counter, yawning. "I'm sorry. What did you want?" She asked for the third time.

Janie came up behind her. "I've got this." She whispered. "Why don't you go home and get some sleep. You're not used to these early bird hours."

She yawned again. "You can say that again…" came out garbled and running together. Janie, knowing Willow as well as she did, understood every word.

"Embry and Marshall are coming over for dinner to talk about their engagement party. At this rate, they're getting frozen pizza."

Willow drove the few miles to the house she'd inherited from her grandfather. It was a comfortable home. Just when she had decided to do some remodeling, her daughter, Embry, announced she was engaged. Her remodeling fund quickly turned into a wedding dress, caterer, and flower fund. Anytime her mind wandered to her daughter and her fiancé, she smiled. They were made for one another. Marshall played minor league baseball. His dream was the majors. Sometimes Willow hoped with him, sometimes against him. If he hit the majors it was nearly a certainty they would move out of the state—seeing Oklahoma didn't have a major-league baseball team.

Marshall's family volunteered to pay for the wedding—they had a huge family and wanted to invite the whole lot. But Willow still had a bit of pride and she had some money tucked aside. New furniture and repositioned walls could wait. Her daughter's happiness would not.

She pulled into her long driveway and let herself in. The dog was dancing in the gated laundry room. Willow was certain she peed in her excitement. The vet called it excitement urination. Willow called it a pain. She grabbed the paper towels and all-purpose cleaner before she opened the gate. She found if she didn't say a word to the dog, the dribble would be a little less. Sometimes not at all. Today was not a "less" day. The puddle grew as Willow got closer. She was almost on top of the dog before she saw why. "Clover. What did you do?"

The dog stilled and crouched down, averting her eyes then quickly looking back to see if she'd been forgiven yet.

Willow sighed. The back door rug was in pieces. Tiny pieces. She chewed up the whole thing. "Bad dog." Clover turned over in a submissive position.

"No, you're not forgiven." Willow let the dog out to finish emptying her bladder and cleaned up the laundry room floor. Once she finished, she let the dog back in then crawled into bed. Clover nuzzled up close and licked the side of her face. Willow giggled. "OK, fine, you're forgiven. But don't do it again."

The warning was useless. If it wasn't a rug being destroyed it was a shoe, or a whole ham, or the screens, or the blinds, or the siding, or any number of things the dog decided to eat. She even managed to chew up a brick. Willow couldn't figure that one out. She'd bought her those heavy-duty chew toys. Not one survived Clover. Still, the dog owned a large piece of her heart.

She fell asleep with a fifty-pound fur ball snuggled up to her.

Willow slept a dreamless, shiftless sleep. Four hours later, she stretched and looked at the clock. "Clover, the kids will be here in an hour. What are we going to feed them?"

She padded to the kitchen and looked through the freezer. "Nothing. I desperately need to grocery shop." She looked in the pantry next. She had three boxes of macaroni and cheese, one SpongeBob SquarePants, one spiral, and one of the regular macaroni. She looked at her dog. "Do you think anyone would notice if I combined them?" She smiled. "You wouldn't, would you?" She rubbed her head.

Her phone was chirping. She looked around for it and realized she'd never taken it out of her purse. "Embry." She listened to the voicemail Embry left then sent a text message of her own. "Thank you, Janie!"

The reply, "You're welcome."

Janie had saved the day, again. She'd let Embry know what was happening so Marshall and Embry picked up dinner.

Willow hopped in the shower and put on some clean clothes. An hour later Marshall and Embry showed up with her favorite Chinese takeout. Steve pulled in right behind them with a pie from the bakery, lemon meringue, Willow's favorite.

The four of them avoided talking about the murder. The engagement party menu was decided upon, the guest list was compiled, the date was set, and the invitations were ordered. After pie and coffee was served, Embry and

Marshall gave her a hug goodbye and left. All in all, a good evening.

Steve lingered over his coffee. "They're good kids. Makes you wonder why some turn out good and others don't."

He was obviously thinking about Karla and Flynn, maybe John too, Willow wasn't sure. She had no idea if Steve had caught up with the young businessman. Karla or John could have decided to take Flynn out of the equation. She nodded. She was thankful. Her daughter was one of the best. She couldn't ask for better.

They moved to her lumpy couch. "Did you talk with John?"

"We've been playing phone tag. He left me a message asking if he could come in tomorrow. He had some tribal business that had to be taken care of this afternoon and evening." He took a drink of his coffee. "He's meeting us at the coffee shop tomorrow around ten. Will that work for you?"

She nodded then yawned. "I took a four-hour nap. You'd think I'd be awake. Then again…" She held up her cup. "…I did make decaf."

"Good. I was hoping that was the case." He sighed. "You know we're going to have to talk to Molly again. Did you know besides being

Karla's aunt, she was John New Moon's babysitter when he was growing up?"

"No! She didn't say a word about that."

"Well, she was. What has she got herself tangled up in?"

"I hope this has nothing to do with her— well, at least nothing more than a niece and a child she helped raise."

"Oh, and the ME's report came in. He drowned. There were traces of lipstick on his shirt color and on his cheek. Waterproof. And it looks as though he was incapacitated with a stun gun or a cattle prod prior to being drowned."

She shuddered. She loved to swim, she loved water. But, the thought of drowning gave her the willies.

"Someone shocked him then held him under."

"So, it could be anyone. It wouldn't take any great strength to hold a compliant victim in water."

"True. We're looking for someone who has access to either of those types of debilitating devices. A man or a woman could have the upper hand in that situation."

"But, who would want to kill him? Just because he was a picky coffee drinker and a jerk?

I don't think so. There must be more to it. But what?" She looked at Steve expectantly.

"How about a love triangle? Either Karla or John have the motive. And both have the strength."

"The question is, do they have an alibi?"

"If either one came back now and said they were with the other, I'd have to wonder who was trying to protect who."

"Or—maybe they really were together and Karla didn't want to admit she ran straight to John after Flynn hit her. Maybe her crying jag was all an act?"

"I guess we wait until tomorrow then and see what John has to say."

Willow yawned again. "Yep. Want to watch a movie?" As tired as she was, the thought of sitting next to him pulled on her like she was a love-sick teenager.

"I would love to, but I won't." He kissed her gently. "You have to get some sleep." He stood up, pulling her with him as he rose. He wrapped her in a hug and just held her. Neither one said a word until Clover jumped up, trying to join in.

"Clover, you jealous beast," She chided. The dog was wedging her way into the hug.

Chapter 5

Willow managed to drag herself out of bed and into the coffee shop by 9:30 a.m. She chuckled. In the afternoon, she called her shop the ice cream shop, mornings were all about the coffee. Her grandfather's ice cream shop had been part of her inheritance, she added on the coffee side to increase revenue. Now, her two favorite things were part of her daily life—and she hadn't grown tired of them yet! Although her jeans seemed to grow tighter by the day.

She poured herself a strong cup of dark roast and added some cream. Pumpkin muffins were on the menu as well as apple spice muffins. She set three apple muffins aside and waited for Steve and John to show up. She liked that Steve was giving John the benefit of the doubt and meeting him away from the station—professional courtesy.

Janie had the cases filled with her latest treats. Beside the muffins, Willow noticed pumpkin bars, apple pie bars, pecan tarts, and sweet potato tarts. Her head dropped. *How am I going to lose weight with all this around me? I have absolutely no will power.* Her mind drifted to her daughter's wedding and she thought about the mother of the bride tent she was going to have to wear. She put one of the muffins back and took a cup of fruit and a yogurt from the cooler. "I can do this."

Willow found Janie working in the office. "I'm placing an order, anything special you want?"

"What do we have to offer the diet-conscious?"

Janie frowned. "Fruit, yogurt..." She paused. "We have those delicious bran muffins you made a few months ago. We could start doing fruit smoothies. Maybe add some greens? Green smoothies are really popular right now. What do you think? Expand our menu a little?"

"Let's do it. Maybe instead of muffins each morning I can have a kale smoothie." The corners of her mouth tipped downward. "I'm going to have to learn to say kale smoothie with a lilt to my voice and twinkling eyes, like when I say, pumpkin muffin. Maybe then I'll believe it's just as good as cream cheese frosting." She stuck out her index finger to swipe a little of the confection from a bowl and Janie smacked her hand.

"That's it. I'm taking charge of your diet— and exercise."

Willow began to panic then took a deep breath. "You're right. Of course, you're right. This is perfect. You can be my accountability partner." She smacked her own head. "Why didn't I think of this before? I mean, you're perfect. You're what a size 8?"

"Um…a 2."

"Oh. I'm not sure I've ever been a size 2. I mean, I was born a firm 10. And I've just grown up from there."

Janie sighed. "Willow, it's not about size. It's about being healthy, feeling good in your own skin, and having energy to spend with your loved ones."

Willow scowled. "Easy for you to say. You're a 2."

"I could be just as unhealthy at my small size. I choose to eat right and exercise, every day." Janie threw the dish towel over her shoulder and removed the bowl of cream cheese from view. "You don't need this temptation."

"Janie, I own an ice cream shop and a coffee shop with the best baked goods in three counties. Am I supposed to close shop?"

Willow was saved from an answer by the sound of the bell followed by Steve's voice.

"Hello. Anyone here?"

"I'm coming." She hollered from the kitchen. She picked up the tray with the muffins and fruit—paused—then quickly added another muffin before hurrying to the table.

Janie yelled. "I saw that!"

Steve bent down and kissed her. "What was that about?"

"Nothing. Not a thing." She placed the tray on the table then went for coffee and told herself, *I promise, I'll start my diet tomorrow.*

A good looking Native American Indian man walked through the door. Steve stood up and shook his hand. "You must be John. I think we may have met at some community function but I can't quite remember." He introduced Willow before sitting back down.

Willow just smiled and sized him up. Was Karla crazy? There wasn't any comparison between John and Flynn. John's smooth complexion, dark eyes, and slightly ruffled bad boy haircut just magnified his natural good looks. His smile lit up the room. He shook Willow's hand—firm, but not hard enough to hurt. She liked him and immediately decided he was innocent. She shook her head slightly to Steve who completely ignored her.

John initiated the conversation. "What can I help you with, Chief?" Willow chuckled but quickly shut her mouth when both men gave her a funny look.

Steve answered. "Flynn Allen was found murdered in Molly's café early this morning. Do you know anything about that?"

John shook his head. "No, I'm sorry, I don't."

"But you already know?"

"Yeah, Karla called me yesterday afternoon. I guess she had just found out about it. She was pretty upset. I was already out of town for my meeting."

"Did you have an altercation with him the evening before at Karla's parents' house? The night of the fall festival?"

He rolled his eyes. "I was invited by Mrs. Mitchell. She told me Karla had come back and would love to see me. She failed to mention Karla brought her fiancé who was there to get her parents' blessing to marry their daughter. Had I known those facts I would never have showed up." He shook his head. "I was only there for a few minutes. As soon as I realized what was going on, I left. Unfortunately, Flynn saw me and pretty much lost it. He left in a rage. I didn't need the drama so I left too."

[43]

"Yet you spent the evening with Karla? Cheering her up?"

He eyed Steve for a moment before answering. "Who told you that?"

"Well, did you?"

John was silent for a brief second. "No. I haven't seen Karla since I left her parent's house."

It was Steve's turn to study John. "How about Flynn? Did you see him again that night?"

"No. I went home and went to bed."

"Can anyone vouch for you?"

"Nope. I was home, alone." He went on, "Look. Karla and I, yeah, we used to be an item. I thought we were going to be together forever. She left with lots of promises about coming back to Oklahoma and us spending the rest of our lives together. That didn't happen. It was a long time ago. I've moved on. So has she. We're two completely different people now." His gaze drifted to the left of Steve and out the front glass window. Karla was standing there, staring back.

The door jingled as Karla entered. "John. I didn't know you were coming into town."

"The Police Chief wanted to talk with me about you and Flynn."

She nodded in observation of the two others seated at the table, but her eyes never left

John's. "When you're done, do you have a few minutes?"

"Sure. I think we're almost done here." He looked to Steve. "Aren't we?"

Steve nodded. "Yeah, just don't leave the area without talking to me first."

John nodded then led Karla to a table on the far side of the shop.

Willow and Steve watched their interaction for a moment before continuing their own conversation.

Willow took a drink of her cold coffee and sputtered. "Well, what did you make of that?"

"I'm not sure yet. The one thing I do know is, they are far from over one another. His countenance completely changed when she appeared at that window."

"Yep. No way can you hide that kind of reaction."

"What gets me is, he didn't even try."

"Nope, he sure didn't." Steve changed the subject. "So, you gonna tell me what you and Janie were talking about when I came in?"

"Girl talk. Nothing to concern yourself with." She took their cold coffee and replaced it with steaming mugs. "John didn't eat his muffin."

"Don't worry. I won't let it go to waste."

Willow scowled. It wasn't fair. How could he eat so much and stay so thin? She'd have to give this weight loss plan a whole lot of thought.

Chapter 6

Willow stared through the window front of the new bookstore on Main Street, just a few stores down from Molly's Café, which was now open and full to the brim. Everyone wanted to get the scoop on what happened. Willow had the scoop so for her it was the book store and the food and health section. There had to be something she could do to lose weight.

She perused the book shelves and started tossing books in her basket.

Atkins. Hmm…meat. I love meat. Cheese. Oh, what I wouldn't do for a good slice of Manchego. Eggs. All my favorites. I can do this.

Paleo Diet. Meats, fish, fruits, and vegetables. I love fruit. I love vegetables.

Carb Cycling. Huh. This might work. Low carb days and high carb days. Confuse your body into losing weight. Like I need more confusion in my life.

Willow hefted the basket onto the checkout counter.

The pretty young woman behind the counter greeted her with a smile. "Research, huh?"

"You could call it that." She eyed the young woman. "You new in town?"

"Yeah. My dad owns this chain of bookstores. I'm here getting this one up and running. We specialize in book stores for small towns. Nothing too fancy and we keep our stock limited to market demand." She had three bags lined up on the counter. "And our prices are very competitive." She looked at the register and gave Willow her total.

Willow flinched a little but she pulled out her debit card. "I can see that."

The clerk extended her hand. "I'm Daisy. Daisy Fisher."

Willow followed suit as she studied the dimpled blond woman standing before her. "I'm Willow Crier. I own the ice cream coffee shop down the street. Welcome to Turtle."

Daisy smiled, fully exposing both dimples on her cheeks and a set of extremely white teeth. Willow nearly looked away.

Willow lugged her bags of books to the car. "I guess I'll do some reading tonight."

A few minutes later she was standing in the kitchen of the coffee shop. "Janie, I don't know. I mean, I'm not sure I'm ready." She closed her eyes. "What are you making?"

"The only way you're going to get ready is just do it. Now, I'll be over tomorrow morning to collect you—right after the morning rush. Josh and Becca will both be in and can take care of the shop." She pointed to Willow. "You and me, tomorrow morning at ten. You better be up and ready."

Janie turned to check on the oven and Willow snatched a pumpkin cheese cake ball from the tray.

"I saw that."

"You did not. There's no way!" She hurried back out to the parking lot and got in her Jeep. She dialed Embry's number. "You free for dinner? I'm coming into the city."

Willow glanced in the back of her jeep. Her first stop had been for good running shoes, thanks to Janie she would be needing those in the morning, and the last stop was Whole Foods for Agave nectar. She hadn't really planned on making the trip but the girl had been through enough. The least Willow could do was make her a decent cup of coffee that didn't upset her stomach. The packages in the back of her jeep were piled high. *Dieting sure is adding to the cost of this wedding!*

Embry was already at the restaurant when Willow arrived. She had already ordered bruschetta. "What brings you to the city?"

"I needed new tennis shoes, some things for the shop, and a few other things. I figured I might as well make the trip. Besides, then I get to see you." She helped herself to some of the appetizer.

"This is good. We need to eat Italian more often."

Willow studied the menu. *I wonder which diet includes Italian.* "Good idea. Good stuff!" She ordered the chicken and mushroom Marsala and an ice tea then rested against the booth.

"Mom, tell me what happened."

Willow recounted the whole story to Embry. "Steve has his hands full. I mean, Flynn is from New York, he's not even from around here. Who has a motive? I highly doubt John would suddenly kill someone for a girl he hasn't seen in five years. Maybe it was a loose cannon who Flynn offended at the grocery store. They say there's always a could-be murderer living among   us."

"Yeah, besides Karla and John, who would have

a reason to?" She sipped her Italian soda. "Molly wouldn't, would she?"

"Molly? No, of course not. Molly can't bring herself to kill the flies that venture in the café. She always has Victor or Juan or one of the other kitchen workers do the dirty deed. How in the world could she kill a man?"

"Well, Karla is her niece. They say blood runs thicker than water."

"I've never understood that. Are they saying non-relatives are water? I mean, I don't get it."

"Mom, it's just a saying. Water is thinner…that's all."

"Huh, still, no. Can't be Molly. It's gotta be someone else."

"Why did they come here? If they hate it so much, why bother? And don't tell me Flynn came to ask for Karla's hand in marriage. He doesn't sound like the type to be into getting anyone's approval."

"You know, Karla never did say why they were in town. I'll have to ask her."

Their meals came and the topic of conversation turned to the engagement party and the wedding.

Embry grew pensive.

"What's on your mind?"

[51]

"I was just wondering if I should invite dad to the wedding."

Willow's fork dropped to the plate. "Why would you want to do that?"

Embry raised her eyebrows slightly. "Well, he's my dad. I know he hasn't been a good one, but, he's still my dad. I'll never get married again. I guess I wouldn't mind him being there, especially if he wants to come."

She raised her eyes to meet her mom's.

Willow looked down at her nearly finished plate of pasta. *Now my appetite leaves me. Why didn't she bring up this topic at the beginning of the meal?* She pushed her plate back. "Well, if that's what you want to do." Her syllables were clipped, leaving no doubt as to her true feelings of her daughter inviting her ex to the wedding.

Embry tightened her mouth. "You know what, just forget it."

Willow softened, slightly. "Embry, that man wanted nothing to do with you. He didn't spend a dime of his money, a minute of his time, or any energy whatsoever in bringing you up. I understand he donated sperm to create you. But he's not your father. Never has been, never will. He doesn't care about anyone but himself. If he comes, he's only going to hurt you. In fact, if you did invite him I doubt he'd show. He'd break your heart."

Embry sighed. "You're right. I know. I just thought, maybe…"

Willow moved next to her daughter and hugged her. "Don't set yourself up. Please?" She closed her eyes then reopened them. "Look, if I thought he would do the decent thing, if he would come and give you away, and be a dad for once, I'd say go for it. But the man hasn't changed. He hasn't." She kissed her cheek. "Baby, I don't want you to get hurt."

"How do you know he hasn't changed?"

"Has he contacted you at all in the past 20 years of your life?"

Embry hung her head. "No."

"Then you have your answer."

Embry leaned into her mother. "I know, Mom."

Chapter 7

Willow was ready when Janie showed up the next morning. She met her at the door.

Janie looked Willow up and down then started laughing. "What are you wearing?"

Willow looked down at her neon pink running gear. "This is top of the line running gear. It's supposed to help me be aerodynamic."

"You plan on flying?"

"Like the wind."

Janie laughed and pointed. "What about that?"

"You mean my belt?"

"Um, yeah, that and…is that a new watch?"

"It's a Fitbit. It works with my phone and tells me how many steps I've taken and how many flights of stairs I've climbed. It's even got GPS on it so I can map out my running route. It's a wealth of information."

"OK, so what all is in your belt?"

Willow pointed to each item. "Water bottle, snacks, pocket for my phone, earphone jack, keys, ID, money, reflectors, sun visor, sweat towel, pepper spray, Taser, sunblock…"

"Willow…"

"The guy at the sporting goods store said I'd need all this."

Janie tilted her head back. "Did you stop to think he might get paid on commission?"

"Hmmm…well, I have it now. Might as well use it." She bent down to do a few stretches. "You ready?"

Janie had on a pair of loose jogging shorts with leggings under them and long sleeve sports top. She held up her keys. "Mind if I leave these in the house?"

"Ha! See, you need a belt too!" Willow took the keys and put them in an extra pocket in her sport belt.

Both ladies finished stretching then took off jogging down the driveway. Within a few seconds all chatter stopped. Just short of a minute, Willow was panting—hard. Two minutes into the run and she was bent half way over standing   still. "Who…would…(breath)…choose…(breath) to…do…(breath)…this? I think…I'm…gonna throw…up."

"Willow, weren't you walking Clover every day? Haven't you been leading up to this?"

Willow replied defensively, "I walk her—every now and again. She runs all over the yard, why do I have to walk her?" She guzzled from her water bottle. "Oh my gosh."

Janie shook her head. "Come on. We'll start out walking."

The two women walked at a much calmer pace. Willow finally caught her breath. "Do you do this every day?"

"I run every day at 3 a.m."

"3 a.m.? Are you crazy?"

"I'm in bed by eight every night. I'm at the shop by five. I must get up that early if I want to exercise. I'm just too tired to do anything by evening."

"How did I not know this? I mean, I know you exercise, but every morning at three? There are days I'm not yet in bed at three."

"I know."

They walked for a two-mile loop. Willow's hips and calves were burning by the time they reached her ranch. And her feet were blistered. "There really has to be a better way."

"Willow, you can choose a different exercise but if you want to lose weight, you're going to have expend some energy. At our age, we have to be purposeful about exercise."

"You're right. I know it. It's just…you know what isn't fair? Steve can eat and eat and eat and he never gains a pound." She pouted. "That is not fair."

Janie raised her eyebrows at her best friend. "Steve may not jog or go to the gym, but he does more physical activity then both of us put together. He still runs his own ranch, he helps at his sister's, he takes care of the lake property, he's the city police chief and he's always going and he's always doing. That counts too." She held out her hand for her keys. "If you don't want to jog, pick something, anything, to get moving, OK? At the very least take Clover for a walk every day. Besides, walking on the pavement will help her nails stay trimmed."

"OK. I promise. I'll do it." She held up her Fitbit and looked at the stats. "We walked over 4000 steps. This thing is awesome."

"Do this every day and make sure you increase the distance once a week. You will lose some weight if you watch what you eat and exercise." She stressed the and.

Willow nodded. "Got it." She got to thinking about the new gym opening. *Maybe a personal trainer will help.*

Janie started to pull away then stopped and rolled down her window. "A young gal named

Daisy stopped by this morning before I left. She said to tell you hi. I also thought you'd want to know she was sitting with Karla and the two of them seemed pretty chummy." She raised her shoulders and shrugged then drove off.

Willow took a long hot shower before leaving for the shop. She'd had some time to read the overviews of a few of the diet books and she decided the Atkins diet was for her. She breakfasted on scrambled eggs and cheese before leaving for work. "I can do this."

As she was driving, her phone rang. Steve. She turned on the speaker phone. "Hey. What are you up to this morning?"

"Is it still morning?"

Willow glanced at her watch. "Yep. We have twenty-three minutes till we hit noon."

"I was calling to see if you wanted to drive out to the Mitchells' ranch with me. I would like to talk with them about the night before last. See if they know anything. It's a long shot, but maybe there'll be something they can tell us. I'm really running into a dead end here."

"Yeah, no problem. Meet me at the shop?"

She and Steve pulled into the parking lot behind the shop simultaneously. "I need to make sure the part-timers showed up. Then we can take off." Willow slowly walked to the back door.

She reappeared with two cups of coffee. "Here you go."

"What's wrong with you? Another ingrown toenail?"

She guffawed. "No, thank heavens. That was the worst. I went jogging, which quickly turned into walking, with Janie this morning. I got blisters for my efforts."

He looked down at her feet. "Did you get new tennis shoes?"

"I did. Aren't they pretty?"

"You know you're supposed to break in new shoes, right? Wear them a little at a time until your feet are used to them?"

"I figure I'll break them in a lot quicker if I just wear them all the time."

Steve just smiled.

Chapter 8

The Mitchells' ranch sat back far off the road in the middle of wide open space. Using the word ranch to describe the house was using the word loosely. It was a white, two story country-style home with a front porch and barn door-style shutters painted a slate gray. The garage, also two stories, was only connected by a breezeway. When Steve pulled in the driveway, Willow glimpsed a pool in the back yard.

"Nice place."

Steve nodded. "Yep, they've done all right. He's in oil."

Willow glanced at Steve. "With John?"

"Competing companies. But, they like one another enough. No bad blood between them." He climbed the one step to the front door and rang the bell. Karla answered.

"Hi. Did you find something out?"

"No, we'd like to talk with your parents. Are they here?"

"Yeah. Come on in."

Willow looked around as she followed Karla. The living room was spectacular. Just looking at the beautiful room made her wish she could remodel before the engagement party. The wide stained wood floors were consistent throughout the open floor plan. All the décor was shades of white and gray with cranberry accents. The fireplace was mammoth and the focal point of the room. Willow strained to see the signature on the artwork above the fireplace. She cranked her neck to look at the kitchen as they made a turn halfway through the open space and sighed.

She stopped and opened the door to the sun room.

Mr. Mitchell rose to greet them while Mrs. Mitchell moved to the kitchen for refreshments. Karla rolled her eyes. "Country to the core." She whispered as she settled into a chaise lounge.

Willow heard the snide remark and looked sternly at Karla, not that she was paying attention. Her fingers moved quickly over the letters on her phone, obviously typing some important message to someone. "Oh, let me help." She followed Miriam into the kitchen. Seeing the kitchen up close might give her some good ideas for her own kitchen.

"Your home is lovely. Who built your home?"

Miriam smiled. "We recently remodeled. Are you looking to build or remodel?"

"I'd like to remodel, maybe next year."

Miriam placed glasses of ice tea and homemade cookies on a tray and led the way back to the sunroom. Steve helped himself. Willow took a glass of tea but politely declined the cookies.

"Thank you."

Steve wiped his mouth then said, "Mr. and Mrs. Mitchell, is there anything you can tell us about Flynn that might help us figure out who would have done this to him?"

The older couple looked at one another then to Steve.

Karla interrupted. "Dad, Mom, you promised."

Mr. Mitchell turned to his daughter. "Karla, surely you can't expect us to be quiet now."

His daughter scrunched up her face but stayed in the room.

"Karla called me last week and asked if she and Flynn could come here. Seems he got himself into quite the pickle back in New York. He worked for a stock broker and uh, decided to save his own bottom and turn state's evidence. The unfortunate part is Flynn took a lot of money from the company too…money that didn't belong to him. Of course, he spent it. Appearances were more important to that boy than being responsible and living within his means."

"Daddy!"

Mr. Mitchell shrugged. "It's true." He went on. "Karla asked if he could hide out here until things settled down. Flynn wasn't too quiet about where he was headed. He was bragging all over the Big Apple. I'm guessing someone followed him here and well, if anyone knows Flynn at all, they know he doesn't have a dime to his name. I would guess whoever did this decided to cut their losses."

"And you have no idea who that someone would be?"

He shook his head. "No, I don't."

Steve looked to Karla. "How about you, Karla? You know who's behind this?"

Mrs. Mitchell spoke for the first time. "Chief Grice, Flynn was the worst kind of human being. If he had any feelings whatsoever for my daughter, he would have separated himself as soon as he knew he was in danger. Instead, he subjects her entire family to whatever wiles he brought on himself simply to save his own hide. I have no use for that kind of man."

[63]

"Mother!" Karla stood up and stomped out of the room.

Miriam didn't bother acknowledging her daughter. "I'm not sorry he's dead. Perhaps now my daughter will be safe. I can only hope and pray that is so."

Willow fully understood the propensity for a parent to protect their own child—whatever the cost. "I'm sorry I protected my child"—no matter by what means—was said by no parent—ever.

Steve stood up. "Thank you for taking the time to talk to me. You've given us a lot of information to check on. I'll make some phone calls to New York and see what I can come up with." He tipped his hat and led the way out to his truck.

Steve kept looking at Willow as he drove. She finally asked, "What?"

"Are you on a diet?"

Her jaw dropped then she quickly shut it.

"You turned down a homemade cookie. You never do that."

She sighed. "I want to lose a few pounds before Embry's wedding."

Understanding crossed his features. "So, that's why you went jogging with Janie."

"Yes, that's why I went jogging and that's why I didn't eat the cookie." She crossed her arms.

"You could have told me. I can help, you know."

She just shook her head and closed her eyes.

Chapter 9

Willow refused to discuss the diet with Steve. It was bad enough she had to subject herself to Janie and Embry's scrutiny. But Steve? No. No way. He dropped her off at the coffee shop still grinning.

Her stomach rumbled as she entered the kitchen and smelled all the fall scents. The baking was finished and Janie was nearly ready to go home for the day. Willow stashed her purse in the office then donned an apron. "Anything I should know?"

"Yeah, Josh has football practice after school. He'll be in around six. Becca should be here by four though, so you'll have help for the early evening rush."

"Great. Did you give any more thought to some healthier food options we can offer?"

"I think we need to offer some sandwiches and salads. Maybe even a soup now that cooler weather is approaching."

Willow smirked. "It's 80 degrees and November. Are we really going to see cooler weather?" She had thought about offering real food, something other than snacks and treats. "You don't think we're going to cut into Molly's business, do you? I don't want her to be negatively affected."

"No, I don't think so. I chatted with her this morning and she said go for it. She doesn't offer trendy foods anyway and it'll be a nice addition to the town's offerings."

"Oh, good. How about during the quiet times tonight, I'll work on some ideas? We can talk about them tomorrow."

"All right. We'll chat then. I've got to run."

Janie hustled out the door and left Willow with the shop. There were a few people sitting sipping on their coffee, but no one who needed her so she opened her laptop. Instead of googling healthy sandwich options, she googled Flynn Allen New York City, NY.

She read all his public information: place of work, arrest, articles about the upcoming trial. *Mr. Mitchell left that part out. I wonder if he was supposed to be under witness protection?*

Customers walked in the door so Willow shut her laptop. She smiled when she saw Daisy and an older gentleman. Willow greeted her as she approached the counter. "Daisy, good to see you again. Janie told me you were in this morning. Two visits in one day."

"I love your coffee. I'm used to coffee in the big city and well, many times when I'm out setting up a new store I must go without. Not in Turtle. I love this little town." Remembering the gentleman at her side, she said. "Oh, where are my manners. Willow, this is my father, Trevor Fisher. Dad, Willow…?"

"Willow Crier." She extended her hand as she took in the gentleman's good looks. He still had a full head of hair, black and gray, mixed in equal proportions and a trendy close cut beard. His cologne nearly had her swooning.

Daisy continued, "He's here to see how the store is moving along." She grinned. "Isn't he handsome?"

Willow felt herself blush and decided to move the conversation forward. "The town of Turtle is glad to have you. Enjoy your visit, Mr. Fisher. What can I get for you?"

She made their gourmet coffees and added a complimentary pumpkin bar for them to share then took it to their table. "The pumpkin bar is on me. A welcome to town gift."

Daisy grinned. "I'll take a bite then let dad have the rest. I try to watch what I eat."

Willow gave her a halfhearted smile, the guilt taking away every morsel of joy she had.

"Enjoy your refreshments. I'm going to get back to work. Let me know if you need anything."

She returned to her search. Something she had just read was niggling at her, something that sounded oddly familiar. She brought the article she read up again and whispered. "Bennie the King Fish is being investigated in conjunction with the investigation Flynn Allen is tied to. Weird." She looked at the father and daughter duo sipping their coffee. "No, couldn't be, could it?" She said quietly. "Trevor Fisher, Benny the King Fish, coincidence, right?" She closed her computer and shook her head. *I've been reading too many conspiracy theories.*

She cleaned out the glass display case and put all the baked goods back in when the unit was sparkling. She wiped down the counters and scrubbed the sinks. Josh and Becca would be thankful for a slow afternoon. Cleaning was a big part of their job, that and keeping the customers happy.

Middle of the afternoon and the place was empty and quiet. She brought a legal pad from her office and googled healthy sandwiches and salads and had a good list of ideas to go over with Janie.

Steve walked in right after Becca arrived. "Good timing, I'm ready for a break." She was famished. Following the Atkins diet at the bakery proved to be equal to a fasting diet. "I need some protein. You got anything on you?"

Steve felt the corners of his mouth pull but he reigned in his smile. "I do not. But, I could run down to the grocery store. Would some cheese and nuts do?"

Middle and high school students were coming in by the droves. "Would you? I need something to keep up with this crowd. Once Josh comes in I can take a real break. Maybe get a cheeseburger?"

"Sounds good. I'll be right back with a little protein to hold you over." He kissed her cheek and left as Willow went behind the counter to make ice cream cones and milk shakes.

Two hours later, her cheese and nut snack was still sitting on the counter after serving 50 students their ice cream treats. Josh took over for her so she could go get something to eat with Steve.

When the two of them sat down at a booth in Molly's Willow was ready to eat everything on the menu. "This is killing me. I'm starving."

"Did you eat the cheese and nuts I brought?"

"No," She snapped then closed her eyes. "I didn't have a chance. I'm sorry. I didn't mean to take it out on you."

"You do know that you could just eat healthy and exercise, then you won't have to go through this dieting junk."

She glared but didn't say a word as Molly approached the table to take their order. She placed two sweet teas on the table then said, "The specials are a bacon cheese burger with sweet potato fries and your choice of dessert and liver and onions with mashed and gravy also served with your choice of dessert. "What'll it be?"

Willow ordered first. "I'll take the bacon cheeseburger. No bun. No fries. No dessert. Can I have a lettuce salad with bacon, cheese, and chopped egg with ranch dressing?"

Molly raised her eyebrows but didn't say a word. She looked to Steve. "And you?"

He looked from Willow to Molly and back to Willow again. He was in an unsure predicament. He really wanted the cheeseburger with the bun, and the fries, and the dessert, but did he dare? He opened his mouth then closed it again.

Molly put her hand on her hip. "I don't have all day. Had a waitress quit on me today.

Said she can't be working where a guy was murdered."

"I'll have the cheeseburger special."

Molly asked, "As is?"

"As is."

"OK. I'll be right out with some bread and butter."

Steve waited until Molly was out of range before he said, "Flynn Allen was not a nice guy. He had a lot of enemies, some of them worse guys than he was. And word has it that a guy by the name of…"

Willow interrupted. "Let me guess, Benny the King Fish."

"How did you know? And yes, he was after him. The police are looking for him now but he's disappeared. He runs a lot of legitimate businesses to cover up his dirty businesses. They have been trying to nail this guy down for a while. The New York PD thinks this Benny fellow owns the financial institution Flynn pilfered from. That alone could have got him killed."

"I did a little googling myself today. I think he may be in town."

Steve was about to take a drink of his tea then put the glass down. "What?"

Willow filled him in on her theory about Trevor Fisher.

Steve's shoulders visibly fell. "Is that all your going on? His name has Fish in it?"

"Steve, come on, think about it. Who opens book stores in small towns across the US? I mean, how would they survive? It's the perfect cover up for money laundering, or drugs, or any number of illegal activities. And you must admit, the Fishers are from New York, his name has Fish in it, and Daisy has been seen hanging out with Karla."

"They know one another?"

"Yep. Janie said they had coffee together this morning. And they were chummy."

"Well, perhaps we should talk to them. It won't hurt."

Willow whispered. "Speak of the devil."

Steve looked up. Trevor and his daughter entered the café and were being seated on the opposite side of the restaurant.

Trevor looked over to find Willow staring. She blushed and he nodded hello.

Steve was spreading butter on his bread. Willow's stomach growled as she dipped her finger in butter and licked it.

Molly brought their plates.

Willow dug in finding it extremely difficult to not look at Steve's sweet potato fries. She loved sweet potato fries. She had to admit, the burger was delicious. As was the salad. "When are we going to talk with them?"

"I think we'll hang out here for a bit. As soon as they leave we'll follow them out and see if they can chat a bit." Steve said in-between bites.

"Sounds good." She took a long drink of her ice tea and spit it back into her glass. "It's sweet. I'm not supposed to have any sugar." She asked Molly for an unsweetened tea and stared as Steve ate his brownie sundae.

"You want a bite?"

"No. I don't."

He pushed the chocolatey dessert away when Daisy and Trevor stood up. "Looks like I'm done anyway."

Willow and Steve casually followed Daisy and her father out of the restaurant, making it seem more like a chance meeting than a planned confrontation.

"Daisy, Trevor, good to see you. May I introduce you to Police Chief Grice?"

Steve extended his hand while watching Trevor's expression. "Trevor Fisher. This is my daughter, Daisy. I own A Bit of Knowledge Book

Store. Just opened down the street. Daisy runs it for me."

"Good to meet you. Welcome to Turtle."

Willow said, "How do you know Karla?"

Daisy stuttered in answering, just enough to be noticed. "We knew each other back in New York. In fact, she's the one who recommended Turtle. She said you needed a great book store."

Willow grinned. "We do. The library is wonderful and we can usually get books in interlibrary loan, but I'd like to build up my own personal library. You'll remember I was in the other day. Nice store."

Daisy nodded and deferred the conversation to her father.

"I'll be here for a few days. Willow, perhaps you'd like to dine with me, show me around the town."

Willow felt Steve tense beside her. She decided it was her civic duty to take Trevor to dinner and show him around Turtle. He'd only be around for a few days. She could learn more about him, about his business, perhaps determine if he was Bennie the King Fish from New York. Surely Steve wouldn't complain. She remembered a time he wanted her to hang out with a redneck opera singer to get to the bottom of a case. "I would enjoy that. Tomorrow night?"

Steve protectively put his arm around her and said, "Why don't we both go? I love to spend time with my girlfriend and get to know new business men in my community. In fact, why don't we invite Molly? She's not seeing anyone, is she?"

Willow wanted to step on his toes but it wouldn't hurt a lick. He was wearing cowboy boots that protected his feet from horses, surely, they would protect him from her. She smiled and sweetly said, "Yes, why don't we? Molly needs some time out among friends." She turned to Trevor. "Is that OK with you?"

He begrudgingly agreed then politely excused himself and Daisy. "We have some more work to accomplish at the book store. We'll see you tomorrow then." He smiled and added. "Probably for coffee earlier in the day."

Steve turned to Willow. "What was that about?"

"I figured it would be a great opportunity to get to know the guy, find out what he's about. You ruined it."

"I'm not letting you hang out with criminals. No way."

"Letting me?"

Steve threw up his hands. "You know what I mean."

Willow hung her head. "Yeah, I do. I can't live without carbs. It's making me ornery."

"Come on. Let's go see what Molly's schedule is like for tomorrow." He held the door open for her.

"Back again?"

Steve answered. "Yes. We need a table for two and your presence tomorrow evening for a double date. You game?"

Molly stuttered. "Um…uh…what do you mean?"

Willow interjected. "It's pertinent to the case. Can you do it or not?"

Steve said, "Molly, get this woman a piece of peach cobbler before she bites all our heads off."

"OK." Flustered, Molly went off in search of cobbler.

Chapter 10

Willow opened her eyes and screamed. "Ahh…"

"Mom. Get up."

"Embry, what are you doing here it's…" She leaned over the night stand and glanced at clock. "…it's 8 o'clock."

"I know. I have stuff to do later but I wanted to go walking with you."

"I'm gonna kill Janie." Willow pulled her pillow over her head.

"Come on, Mom. I drove all the way over to go walk with you. Now get up. Hurry up."

"My feet are blistered."

"Put Band-Aids on."

"My hips hurt."

"They'll toughen up."

"My workout clothes are dirty."

"Mom, I'm gonna get a cup of water."

"I'm up. Sheesh. And remind me to take away your key."

"What if you fall down and hurt yourself? Who's going to come in and save the day?" Embry replied as she left the room.

Five minutes later Willow stumbled out of the bedroom in a pair of sweats and a T-shirt. She dropped onto the couch and put her tennis shoes on. "Ready?"

Embry already had Clover on her leash. "Yep. Let's go."

Willow was silent as they walked. She didn't go to bed until 3 a.m. and five hours wasn't enough sleep. She couldn't wait to crawl back into bed when she got back.

"Clover, walk nice. Mom, you need to take her to obedience school. She has no idea how to walk on a leash."

Willow mumbled, "You need to go too."

"What did you say?"

"Nothin'."

"Um, Mom, where's your exercise belt?"

"Smarty pants."

Embry laughed then moved to the middle of the country road. Experience told her she was about to get whacked.

By the time they reached the ranch Willow was at least personable. "Hey, does the restaurant have a lot of reservations on the books tonight?"

"No, I don't think so, why?"

"Steve and I are bringing Molly and another guy to eat. Would you make a reservation for me for 7 p.m.?"

"Sure."

She kissed her cheek. "Thanks, Baby." She unlocked the door, took the leash, and closed the door on Embry.

Three hours later Willow finally rolled out of bed. The first thing she did was call Embry. "Sorry about this morning. But a heads up would have been nice."

"Yeah, I'm sorry about that. I'll call next time, OK?"

"You know, I'll start walking Clover every day before I go to work, will that do?"

"Mom, you know I love you just the way you are, right?"

Willow sighed. "I know. Maybe I'm having a hard time loving me. They say that women who overeat use food as a vice. Honey, I just like food."

"Self-discipline mom. That's the key."

"All right. I'll see you in a while. We're going to do an afternoon tour of Turtle and Oklahoma City first. Any suggestions?"

"Hmm…well, your reservation is for seven tonight, so maybe go to Bricktown and take a water taxi? Just drive through the city. It's so spread out and there are so many districts a lot of people don't even know about. Drive by the

Chesapeake Center and the Botanical Gardens. I'd say the number one thing is show them the Oklahoma City National Memorial. But do that first because, well, it's sad. I cry every time I go."

"Thanks, Em. I'll work up a route and see you later, OK?"

Willow wanted to talk to Molly one more time before dinner. Not a formal questioning since Steve wouldn't be present, but, sometimes a gal lets down her guard with friends. Not that Willow ever considered Molly the murderer. But, she very well may know something that she didn't think important to the case. Time has a way of allowing the brain to process and remember information.

Molly had the afternoon and evening covered for the café so she was home getting ready for her blind date. After getting ready Willow invited herself over.

Steve borrowed his sister's Escalade for the evening and promised to pick them up at Molly's. The four of them would have had a difficult time fitting in his truck.

She wore her dressy watch instead of her Fitbit. She still had two hours before the four of them would leave. Willow would have plenty of time to draw some information from her.

Molly opened the door. "Look at you, all gussied up!" She admired the brown pantsuit Willow wore. The color complimented the shade of her auburn hair.

"You're not looking too bad yourself!" Willow replied. In fact, Molly was downright beautiful. She'd never seen Molly look so good. Since breaking up with the barbecue restaurant dude, Molly had kept a pretty low profile. Willow wanted to ask, but thought it rude so she didn't. She hoped Trevor Fisher wasn't involved in this murder. She was rethinking their decision to involve Molly in this. She could get her heart broken all over again. "You dyed your hair. It's gorgeous."

"I did." She touched her hair. "It's not too much, is it? Am I being too obvious?"

"Oh, my goodness no. Molly, it's lovely. Have you lost weight?"

"I have. Thirty-seven pounds. I didn't think it was enough for anyone to notice yet."

"I guess everyone's been so preoccupied with both the fall harvest festival and now the murder I haven't noticed until now. You look fantastic."

Molly positively beamed from the praise. Willow sighed. She'd get there too, she was positive.

The bungalow was adorable. Three bedrooms, two and a half baths, and everything was decorated in light, airy colors contrasting with rich antique side pieces. The overstuffed furniture hugged a person, making them hesitant to leave the comfort of home. Willow chose one such chair to lose herself in.

"Molly, I love your furniture. I'm not sure I want to leave." She put her feet up on the matching ottoman. "I could seriously take a nap."

"That is my favorite place to read."

Willow could see that. Especially in the winter. Placed in front of the fireplace the chair made a wonderful spot to roost. "You want to sit here? I can move."

"No, I'm good." She sat down across from Willow. "So, let me guess. You want to know everything you can find out about the Mitchells, John New Moon, and Karla. I know nothing about Daisy or Flynn so I can't help you there."

"I never could get anything past you, could I?"

"I've been racking my brain for anything that could be relevant. I want this murder solved too. Although business has been crazy busy. People are so nosy. I thought I might have to cancel for tonight. Just because of increased traffic. Everyone working assured me they would handle it fine."

"Did you think of anything?"

"No, not really. But, then again, I guess relevance can vary depending on the variables."

"True. So, why don't you just tell me about the Mitchells first?"

Molly's parents willed the land to both Molly and her brother, Stan. They split the land down the middle and a few years back, when she dreamed of opening a café, she sold most of her acreage to her brother.

When Molly married, her husband worked for the city government, certainly not a job to make one rich, but they lived a comfortable life. Stan on the other hand ended up in oil and profited greatly from the oil boom that Oklahoma prospered from. Her brother and sister-in-law ran in different social circles, went to a different church, lived in a higher income bracket, and had more influence in the community than Molly did. But, they were still family.

Molly blurted, "Miriam has cancer." Sadness flickered across the woman's face. "It's terminal. She and Stan decided quality of life is more important to them than quantity. Stan's taken a leave of absence and they are going to spend as much time as they can together. I really thought that was why Karla came home when she did." She brushed away a tear. "I didn't want to talk about this. I already put my mascara on."

"I had no idea. No one said a thing. How awful."

"Mmhmm." Molly shook her head. "I don't think she has more than six months left, maybe less. Karla is acting like a spoiled little brat. Of course, she is an only child and was given more than enough mercy as a child. Not that Stan and Miriam let her act out. She was still raised with manners. She's just not using them these days."

Willow didn't know what to say. Embry went through stages but most of the time she was a great daughter, better than Willow had been at that age. She decided to change the subject.

"So, how do you know John New Moon? I had no idea you babysat him when he was younger."

Molly nodded, "Yes, I helped out in an afterschool program for kids. He was with from first grade all the way through primary school. He was like a son to me."

"Is he still?"In some ways, yes. He's grown up and like most boys they gain their independence and lose the attachment to their mothers', or in this case, their babysitters' apron strings. He knows he can call on me any time. No matter what it is." She scowled. "I don't know how Karla could have got caught up with Flynn. He was a snake in the grass." She looked to Willow who showed concern. "I didn't kill him. Goodness. Not that it didn't cross my mind a time or two." She let the corners of her mouth tilt up.

The knock at the door ended their conversation. Steve had picked up Trevor on his way to Molly's. Both men were looking good, really good, and Willow couldn't help but stare at Steve. He captured Willow's attention and held it. If Trevor thought she was up for grabs he now knew differently. She only had eyes for Steve.

Molly on the other hand extended her hand as recognition lit her face. "You're Daisy's dad. I met you the other night when you came in for dinner." She tapped Willow on the arm. "I had no idea Mr. Fisher was coming with us."

"Please, call me Trevor."

Molly draped her light wrap around her shoulders with Trevor's help and said, "Are you ready then? We're giving you a grand tour of Turtle, right? It'll take all of two minutes."

He laughed. "I think I've seen everything there is to see here. I'm really interested in seeing some of the city."

"Well, we can make that happen. Can't we?" She asked no one in particular as she led the way to the SUV.

Willow had planned on sitting in the back with Molly so Steve could talk with Trevor but things didn't quite work out the way she had planned. Molly took a shinin' to Trevor and Trevor hit it off with Molly. They both got in the back seat before Willow had a chance. The only good thing was they both talked non-stop. After visiting the memorial which caused both ladies to shed a few tears, Bricktown, the Chesapeake center, and strolling through the botanical gardens, Willow led them into Flint, the restaurant Embry worked at where they were seated near the fireplace.

"This is a lovely restaurant." Molly looked around. "Nothing like my place, is it?"

Trevor patted her hand. "There is room for Barnes and Nobles and room for my little bookstores. Everything has a purpose."

She smiled at him with adoring eyes. Willow flinched. *What if he's a murderer?*

After ordering a charcuterie and drinks, Molly once again opened the conversation with questions for Trevor. "So, do you have brothers and sisters?"

"I have one brother, Benjamin. He's the black sheep of the family."

Willow kicked Steve and raised her eyebrows. Maybe Trevor isn't the King Fisher after all. Maybe his brother, Benjamin is!

Embry brought their entrees and placed them before the group. Willow introduced her daughter all around before she started eating. She ordered the salmon, which came with truffle mashed potatoes and braised swiss chard. She took a bite of the potatoes and smiled. *I'll start my diet tomorrow.*

Chapter 11

Willow woke a half hour earlier than normal to fulfill her promise to walk Clover before going in to work. *Only 11 more days and it'll be a habit.* The dog saw a rabbit and about pulled her arm out of its socket.

By the time she reached the coffee shop, she had a whole new diet plan in place. She had a sack lunch with her so she wouldn't starve by the end of the day. She was going vegetarian. Or vegan. She couldn't remember the difference.

Her smile was contagious as she walked into the kitchen.

Janie had a green smoothie ready for her boss. "Here, I told you I'd have breakfast ready for you. It's got everything you need to get off to a healthy start. I've already sold six of these this morning. And they aren't cheap."

Willow took a drink. "Not too bad. It's actually good. I was a little scared, I'll admit it."

"There's a lot of fruit in it. That's why it's so pricey. The fruit sweetens it up and balances out the bitterness of the greens."

"I think you've got a winner."

"Did you walk Clover this morning?"

"Yes, I did. She about killed me."

She put her lunch in the fridge, washed her hands, then went to check on inventory in the display case. She should have known Janie would have already filled it.

In the corner, Karla Mitchell was nursing a cup of coffee and a yogurt. The young woman didn't seem to be too upset. She was texting and smiling. Willow walked to her table.

"Can I join you?"

Karla looked at the door. "I'm meeting someone…"

"Just for a couple of minutes. I just have a question to ask you."

She nodded to the chair opposite her. "Go ahead."

"How close are you and Daisy Fisher?"

Karla scowled. "We're not. I don't know how you got the idea we are."

"Janie saw you two talking like you know each other well."

"Oh, we know each other all right. But we're not close."

"Daisy said it was your idea for her to open the bookstore here in Turtle."

Karla rolled her eyes. "Yeah, right. It was Flynn's idea. She had a thing for him. They used to date before he fell in love with me. I guess he still felt responsible for her. I don't know why. She's such a daddy's girl."

"May I ask what color and brand of lipstick you use?"

"That's a weird question. I don't wear lipstick. I'm allergic."

"Hmm, OK. Well, it would help the police chief out if you'd tell him the truth about where you were the night Flynn was murdered."

A deep voice sounded behind Willow. "She was with me."

Willow turned around to see John New Moon standing behind her.

How did I miss the bell? "I thought you both said you were alone? Did you concoct this story to provide each other with an alibi?"

"No. We didn't kill him. After he stormed out of my parents' house John caught up with me. I was walking, trying to clear my head." She took his hand. "We knew instantly. The connection, the link between us wasn't broken. It never had been. We just…got lost somehow. I called Flynn and asked him to meet me at the café. I wanted to break up with him and return his ring. He was angry. He did hit me. But, I broke up with him because he just wasn't the guy for me. I'd been under some kind of trance, living in some alternative world. It's like…coming home woke me up." She smiled up at John.

Willow watched the two young people stare into each other's eyes. She wasn't going to get any more information from them now. Two sick little love birds.

She excused herself from the table then called Steve from the office and told him about her conversations with Karla and John and Molly from the night before.

After prepping cookie batter for the morning, Willow worked in the office paying bills and catching up on paperwork while her part-timers waited on customers.

After a couple of hours of paperwork, her stomach started rumbling. She was eating at her desk when Embry stopped by. "Hey, Mom."

"Hey, your day off?"

"Um Mom, I thought you were on a diet?"

Willow looked down at her food. "I am."

"Mom, you're eating chocolate cake."

"Oh, no, it's OK. I've decided that vegan is the way to go."

"So, you're eating cake?"

"Yeah, isn't it great? It's like, diet chocolate cake. I didn't even know such things exist." She looked incredulous. "I mean, this is the diet for me. I feel so much better already. I think it's working."

Embry shook her head. "OK, um, I need to talk to you."

She pointed to the chair across from her desk. "Sit. Talk. I'm all ears."

"I called dad."

"Embry, I thought we had this discussion." She set her fork down. "As a matter of fact, we did have this discussion."

"Mom, you said if you thought he'd follow through you'd be all for it. Well, he wants to be a part of the wedding. He wants to have a part in it. He's willing to help pay for it even."

"Did he already send you a check?"

"Mom!"

"Well, did he? Because he's made lots of promises in the past and guess what, he never follows through. Embry, when are you going to trust me?"

"Mom, it's not about trusting you. It's about having my dad walk me down the aisle."

"I thought I was going to walk you down the aisle?"

"Mom, you're my mom, not my dad."

"Well, someone should have told me that 23 years ago, when I had to be both."

Embry started crying. "Can't you try to understand?"

"I'm trying. I really am."

"I gotta go."

Willow watched her daughter leave then panicked and went after her. "Embry, stop. I'm sorry, OK? I just see this ending a very different way than you do. I don't want you hurt, Baby."

"Mom, you can't save me from ever getting hurt. It's part of life. But you have to believe in me more. You raised me to be strong, to be capable. If he doesn't follow through, yeah, I'll be hurt. But I'll be OK because I know I have you."

Willow clung to her now sobbing daughter. "I know you will. It's OK, honey. If he messes everything up, we'll be here to pick up the pieces. We've done it before. We can do it again."

"Maybe this time he won't."

"Maybe not. I sure hope not."

Chapter 12

Willow decided to up the distance she was walking Clover in the mornings. She was still eating vegan—second day in a row and the longest she'd held out on any diet—and feeling great. As far as she could tell the only problems she encountered was the cravings for a hamburger, or a steak, well, meat of any kind really, and the fact she'd gone up two pounds. She was beginning to think vegan might not be the best way to lose weight. She bought a bunch of vegan groceries. There was vegan bread, pasta, even cake and cookies. She sighed. She decided to stick it out and see if things got better—at least for a day or two.

Willow pulled in front of the new book store, anxious to see what color lipstick Daisy wore. Steve called that morning with an update.

She bounced in smiling, hoping to catch Daisy off guard. The petite blond met her with a smile. "Back for more diet books?"

"Nope. I'm going vegan."

"Oh wow, you have more will power than me."

"I doubt that. I mean, there's a lot you can eat being vegan."

"You do know that eating vegan isn't necessarily a diet, right? You can still over eat and gain weight eating vegan. Granted, in many ways it's a healthier way of eating but you still have to watch what you eat."

Willow cringed. Not what she wanted to hear. She changed the subject. "Daisy, what is that lipstick you're wearing? It's gorgeous!"

"Isn't it though? It's Backstage Bambi by Kat Von D. You can get it at Sephora, in the mall."

Willow's eyes widened. "I'm not sure if I could wear it with my skin tone, but it's beautiful on you."

She smiled. "Thanks. I love it."

Willow walked around the store. Once she was out of Daisy's sight, she sent a text off to Steve. She sought out pet care books while waiting for Steve.

He joined her a few minutes later. "I hate this."

"I know. But, it's definitely her lipstick on his shirt collar and on his cheek. She may not have killed him but she was certainly with him the night he was killed. And they were at the very least kissing."

"Let's go talk to her." Steve led the way to the counter. "Hi, Daisy. I'm gonna need you to answer a few questions for me."

"OK, I'll help with whatever I can."

Steve nodded. "Why did the ME find your lipstick on Flynn's shirt collar and cheek?"

She gave Willow a dirty look. "I should have known you weren't being friendly."

Willow sighed. "If it makes you feel any better I was really hoping your brand didn't match."

"Fine. Yes, I was with him at the café. Weird place to meet but I guess it works. He had just broken up with Karla and needed a friend. So, I obliged. Things got a little out of hand but hey, he was free. He was alive when I left him, I swear he was."

"Was it Karla or Flynn that encouraged you to open a bookstore here in Turtle?"

Her eyes nervously glanced around. "Yeah, OK, it was Flynn. He wasn't married to her yet. He was only using her to get away from my uncle."

Steve asked, "Your uncle?"
"Yeah, my uncle owned the company Flynn worked for. He got himself in some real hot water with him, my uncle's not really a nice guy, and Karla got her parents to agree to let him hide

[97]

out at their place. They barely gave in. If he'd have broken up with her they would never have given him a place to hide."

"Did your uncle know you dated Flynn?"

"Look, I date a lot of guys. Maybe that's one of the reasons Flynn and I got along well. We have the same philosophy in life: C'est la vie. We do what we feel like doing, especially when it comes to relationships. Ours wasn't serious, Chief Grice. It was convenient. Nothing more. If I was back in New York, I'd be with someone else. He happened to be here and be available. There's not much more to it than that. So, to answer your question, my uncle would never try to keep up with the guys I date. There's no point. I'm usually on a different guy's arm every night of the week." She shrugged.

Willow shuddered. She couldn't imagine that kind of attitude. Yet, so many young girls thought the way Daisy did. She wondered if she had a mother in her life. Her dad didn't seem the type to model that kind of living.

"Oh, I can see the wheels spinning. Please, don't bother judging me. I know I'm in the Bible belt. My life is more common than you think. We don't go for the get married, have babies, submission kind of life. We're a new generation."

Willow didn't say a word. She didn't have to. Her face said it all.

Chapter 13

Steve followed Willow back to the coffee shop where Willow poured them both a cup of coffee. "That is so sad. No wonder she wasn't showing any grief. I really didn't think she was the one with him that night, she wasn't upset, at all. He didn't mean a thing to her."

"If she didn't care about him, why would she kill him? What would her motive be?"

Willow shook her head. "I have no idea. It takes a lot of passion to kill someone. Daisy just doesn't care enough, does she?"

"No. It doesn't seem that way. Of course, she could be putting us on. I don't want her leaving town but I really don't think she did it." He sipped his coffee. "I think we need to go back and talk to the Mitchells. In light of her having cancer and Karla and John getting back together, I want to see how they're reacting to all this."

She tipped her cup as she stood up. "Wait for me. I'm coming too."

Steve and Willow pulled up to the Mitchell ranch amidst a flurry of activity. "Wonder what's going on?"

"Let's find out." Willow climbed out of the truck and asked she first person she met.

"Why, a wedding. That's what. Ms. Karla and Mr. New Moon are gonna tie the knot."

Willow turned to Steve who heard the reply. "Well, well. Let's go talk with the family of the bride, shall we?"

Steve knocked on the door but the noise level was so high no one noticed.

"I don't think they're gonna care if we just walk in, do you?" The large inside door was already open so Willow grinned and opened the glass outside door. "Everyone else is just walking in." She led the way, looking around as she walked.

A team of florists were arranging flowers both in the house and in the back yard. With Embry's wedding coming up Willow was more interested in the wedding preparations than she was in finding the Mitchells. She started collecting business cards from all the workers. "Steve, look, isn't that tent awesome? You could even have heaters in that thing."

"Do you see Stan or Miriam Mitchell yet?"

"Oh, I wasn't looking. Sorry. I figure I'll run across them sooner or later. In the meantime, I'm getting some great ideas." She hurried over to back door to watch the commotion—A three-piece ensemble was practicing. "How quaint. I love that idea. Wonder where they found them."

Mrs. Mitchell walked through the French doors into the living room. "Police Chief Grice, Willow, what can I do for you?"

Willow turned toward her but played dumb. "What's going on?"

Miriam's excitement was contagious. "Haven't you heard? John proposed and Karla accepted. They decided they didn't want to chance losing one another again so they decided they weren't going to wait. I'm so excited I can hardly stand it. To think, I'm gonna see my baby get married before…" She paused. She ended with, "…Only good thoughts today."

"I see. Congratulations. My daughter's engagement party is in December, so I may have to get with you later for some advice."

"Of course, I would love that." She grew serious. "Um, if you didn't come to wish us congratulations, what did you come for?"

Instead of answering her question Steve asked, "When is the wedding?"

"Tomorrow afternoon and we have a million things to do."

"Why don't we talk after the wedding? Are the kids getting away for a honeymoon?"

"They are. Only for a couple of days though. Since this is last minute John could only take off a couple of days from work. They'll go on a longer honeymoon later. Probably after Christmas."

"All right, let's plan on meeting day after tomorrow."

She placed her hand on Steve's arm. "Thank you. You have no idea how much that means to me." Her face brightened. "Why don't you two come? We'd love to have you." Seeing doubt cross Steve's face, she added, "A last minute wedding isn't often well attended. We need more bottoms in the chairs. Truly, we do."

Steve agreed to attend after watching Willow's face light up. "OK, we'll come. Is the couple registered?"

"No, they'll just be happy to have people attend."

After getting the specifics Steve said, "Well, we'll see you tomorrow then." He led Willow back to the truck.

"We're going to a wedding. How do you put a wedding together in such a short amount of time?"

Steve shook his head. "I have no idea. I've never had one."

Willow smiled and didn't say another word.

Chapter 14

Willow rummaged through her closet looking for something suitable—and something that fit—to wear to the wedding. She was knee high in boxes at the back of her closet when she heard her phone chirp.

"Oh bother!" She moved as fast as the crammed space would allow and she still missed the call. "Molly." She called her back and agreed to meet her at the café in an hour then went back to her quest.

One box produced a lovely skirt and top combination that would work perfectly. She tried them on, hoping against hope they would fit. The blouse was loose enough and fit fine, but the skirt wouldn't button. She pulled out her miracle working, fat blasting, inch reducer from the top drawer of her nightstand. "Tonight, you will work your magic!"

After smelling the clothes and nearly gagging from the combination of mothballs and card board box scent, she tossed the long flowery maxi skirt and the long sleeve bohemian blouse in the washing machine. Combined with sandals the outfit was exactly what she was looking for—provided the miracle working purchase actually worked.

"Hmm, now to meet Molly." She tucked her purse under her arm, gave Clover a pat then left the house in a hurry. If she had time she desperately needed a manicure.

She met a tearful Molly in the restaurant. "Molly, what's the matter?"

"She's been arrested? Steve arrested her."

Willow knew nothing of this new development. "Who? Who did he arrest?" *Surely it can't be Karla! What a wedding that would be!* Willow thought to herself as she waited for the answer.

"Daisy. He's arrested Daisy."

Willow looked at her funny. "Well, he probably had a good reason."

"No, I'm sure she didn't do it."

"How can you be so sure?" Willow was fairly certain the girl didn't do it either but she wanted to hear Molly's reasoning.

"I just am. And Miriam called me and wants me to put together food for tomorrow's wedding. It's all too much. I can't do it. I need help."

Willow sat Molly down. "Tell me why it can't be Daisy."

"Trevor and I are just getting to know each other. I like him, Willow, I really do. This will ruin everything." She sobbed.

Willow scrunched her eyebrows. She was hoping for something a little more concrete. No such luck. "Well, maybe he just took her in for questioning."

"Nope, Trevor called me and said he's getting a lawyer. He wouldn't need one if Daisy was just being questioned, would he?"

"Sometimes people want their lawyers with them just to make sure there is no coercion or so their rights aren't compromised. It doesn't automatically mean she's been arrested. Why don't I head to the station and see what's going on, OK? And do you want some help for tomorrow? I can make some phone calls. I bet Embry would help if she has off."

"Would you? Oh, Willow. I knew I could count on you."

First thing Willow called Embry. "You busy tonight and tomorrow?"

"I'm off both days. What do you need help with?"

She explained the wedding and the need for help. Embry volunteered both her and Marshall, who was on break from the baseball season, and both wanted to earn a little extra cash for their honeymoon. They picked out a lovely little cottage overlooking the Atlantic Ocean on St. Thomas Island. Embry had shown her pictures and Willow hoped someday she would go someplace romantic with someone she loved. The place even had its own splash pool, right on the side of a cliff with phenomenal views. And if she didn't go with that special someone, she decided she'd go alone!

Embry interrupted her dreaming. "We'll be there in an hour. Can I get you anything?"

"Bring some nail polish. My hands look horrid. Maybe after we finish up helping Molly cook you can give me a manicure."

After talking with Embry, she headed to the police station and Steve's office.

"What happened? You arrested Daisy?"

"I did. I'm following the evidence. The hair on his clothing has her DNA. It's her lipstick on his clothes and skin. She has already admitted she was with him at the café. She has no other alibi for the time of the murder. She owns a stun gun. And I have witnesses in New York who will swear he meant a whole lot more to her than she is letting on. He dumped her in New York for Karla. Hell hath no fury…"

"Yeah, I get it." She sat down on the chair across from him and sighed. "How do I get mixed up in these things? Life was so much simpler before I became the whodunit queen."

He smiled. "You enjoy solving crimes, don't deny it."

"But I don't like murder." "No, only creeps and psychos like murder. You just happen to be good at solving them."

"I guess that's it then. The murder has been solved."

"Don't be sore because you didn't figure it out this time. We can take turns, you know."

Willow scowled.

"Besides, you haven't heard the best part yet. She had a large sum of money deposited in her personal account given to her by her uncle. What was that for?" He didn't wait for an answer. "I'll tell you what it was for. He ordered a hit on Flynn and he knew she could get close to him. Like Uncle, like niece."

Willow grimaced. "I'll admit the evidence is pretty condemning. Did she confess?"

He shook his head. "She insists when she left he was alive and well. Happy in fact. And he didn't care one bit about that ring in the tub. He said he'd bought it at a pawn shop. It was fake."

Willow gasped. "You're kidding."

"Nope. I've asked for the ring to be assessed. We'll know soon if she's telling the truth."

"What did she say the money her uncle gave her was for?"

"Supposedly it was an investment. She's thinking about opening a gym here in Turtle. Did you hear anything about that?"

"As a matter of fact, I did. You haven't?"

"No, who did you hear it from?"

"I'm sure it was someone at the shop. You know, I hear stuff from everyone. I don't remember who specifically but I was thinking if it did open, I might hire a personal trainer." She realized she opened herself up for dieting advice so she quickly changed the subject. "I have a funny feeling there's something Molly isn't telling us."

"Like what?"

"I don't know." She looked up. "Speaking of Molly, she's doing the catering for the wedding tomorrow. She's freaking out so Embry and Marshall are coming over to help cook. You want to spend the evening with us? Maybe we can get Molly to tell us what she knows." She knew how to get a commitment out of the man.

He glanced at his watch. "I still need to get my suit ready for tomorrow. Are you cooking at the café?"

"Yeah. I'm gonna head home to feed Clover then I'll be back. I think the kids are just going to crash at my house tonight since they have to be back early tomorrow."

Steve met Willow in the parking lot and held the door open for her to enter the café.

Molly pulled Willow aside and asked, "What's he doing here?"

"He's come to help. Embry and Marshall will be here any minute too." Willow studied Molly's face. She was genuinely upset. "Molly, why don't you want Steve here?"

At that moment, Trevor came from the kitchen wearing an oversized chef's apron. He stopped in his tracks. "What's he doing here?"

"Oh, now I get it." Willow looked from Trevor to Steve and back again.

Steve just raised his eyebrows. "I'm here to help a friend. You have a problem with that?"

Willow had no idea inviting Steve to help would cause so much conflict. Had she known that Trevor would be there helping she never would have invited him. She knew when Trevor walked through the kitchen door there would be trouble.

"Steve and I can assemble cheese platters here in the dining room…"

Molly caught on, "…Trevor and I can work on the potatoes in the kitchen. Perfect." She took Trevor's arm and led him back to the kitchen.

A few minutes later Molly reappeared with large wedges of cheese and long rolls of sausage. "I'm sorry, Steve. I didn't mean to sound unthankful for your help. I just didn't want there to be problems. I have enough to worry about."

He gave her a quick hug. "If it's causing you too much stress I have plenty of work I can be doing at home. Won't offend me at all if you want me to go."

"I think it's OK. I'll talk to Trevor. You're only doing your job. Even though we know she didn't do it." She gave him a sly glance before going back toward the kitchen.

"I won't quit looking, I promise. You believe me, right? Even though the evidence is pointing in her direction, I know it doesn't always tell the whole story."

"I know you'll be fair Steve. You always are." She turned to Willow, grateful. "When Embry and Marshall get here would you send them in the kitchen? I'm going to have them make the vegetable trays."

"Will do."

After Molly went back in the kitchen Steve said, "A warning might have been nice."

"If I had known he was going to be here I would have said something. They just met a week ago and had their first date the night before last with us. How was I to know they were already to this point in their relationship?"

He pulled her close. "I'm sorry. I guess this case is stumping me. I don't like where it's going and I can't do anything about it."

"We'll figure out what happened. Someone had to have seen something. Let's just get this food prepared. One thing at a time, right?"

Together they worked until all the food was either prepared or prepped. Exhausted, they set out for Willow's place, sans Steve who was heading home to collapse.

After returning home and getting Marshall settled in the guest room, Willow pulled out her miracle box and showed it to Embry. "I need your help."

"What do you have here?" Embry took the box from her and began reading. "Mom, where did you get this? I've never heard of this brand."

"Well, I found it online and ordered it. I've been waiting to try it and what better time than the present? Besides, the skirt I want to wear doesn't fit. This will make all the difference."

"I'm not sure this is a good idea. I've never even heard of this brand."

"Oh, it's fine. It was a lot cheaper than the more popular brand. If it doesn't work, I'll find something else to wear. How's that?"

"OK, but I've heard these can, well, they can cause some problems. They don't always work and they can cause skin irritation, especially on sensitive skin." She paused to see if her mother was listening.

"Let's just try it. What can go wrong?"

Embry rolled her eyes and opened the package then helped her mother apply the fat soaking wrap to her waist line. "This has to stay on a minimum of 45 minutes. We can do our nails while it works."

"Won't it work better if I leave it on all night?"

"Mom…"

"Come on, let's do our nails. I can do yours first."

The next morning Willow removed the wrap to find herself in a mad state of itching and little red blotches all over her middle. "Embry. Oh no. I must have left it on too long."

"Do you think?"

They applied anti itch medication and hoped for the best. The smile on Willow's face as she buttoned her skirt with ease made the itching all worthwhile. "See, it worked!"

Chapter 15

The forecast was sunny and beautiful. A not too hot 65-degree high would be perfect for a lovely afternoon wedding, at least in Willow's opinion. Although Willow, originally being from the north enjoyed the cooler weather, many Oklahomans would be chilly. Embry had talked her into wearing a shorter, more form fitting top that showed off her lost flab. Not short enough to reveal skin, she wasn't a teenager, but certainly not flowy enough to hide what was there. She felt good, young, sexy.

Embry and Marshall were helping Molly's crew set up the food. The menu was simple fare. Mostly finger foods, and everyone would be free to enjoy the actual ceremony.

Molly, still stressed from both Daisy being arrested and having to cater a last-minute wedding, seemed to be running in circles. Willow excused herself from conversation and went to help.

She took Molly's hand. "Come here." After moving to a private spot on the side of the house Willow helped her calm down. "I'm no longer here as a guest. I'll be helping you. Now, settle down. Everything is going to be all right."

Stan Mitchell chose that moment to walk around the corner. "Molly, is everything OK? I know we asked you to help out but I don't want you stressed at your own niece's wedding."

Molly was taking deep breaths so Willow responded. "A lot has been happening. It's a little overwhelming. Between catering a last-minute wedding and Daisy getting arrested for murdering Flynn…"

Stan interrupted. "Wait a minute, Daisy was arrested?"

"Yeah, the evidence is overwhelming but she keeps insisting she didn't do it. Steve is wanting a cut and dried case. He needs a confession from her which isn't happening. Now she's lawyered up." Willow shup up. She realized she'd been talking non-stop. "Enough about all that. I'm going to step in and help Molly. I'll be in my seat in time for the ceremony."

Stan's face dropped. Willow didn't know what everyone's problems were but she needed to get a detailed list of what still needed to be accomplished. She ushered Molly into the Mitchell's kitchen and got the to-do list. She left Stan alone to handle his own problems.

Molly was still turning in circles when Willow and the rest of the crew had the food laid out. Willow was concerned. Molly usually had it all together. Not today. Willow was certain something else was affecting Molly's ability to function. She didn't have time to worry about that. The wedding was about to start.

Willow slipped into her seat next to Steve and smiled. "I'm glad I didn't miss anything."

"Nope, not a thing."

Willow was growing uncomfortable. The itching was mind blowing and somehow her skirt felt like it was getting a little tighter. *Impossible. Maybe I'm bloating. The results are supposed to last a couple of months, at the minimum.*

Together they watched Stan, whose smile refused to reach his eyes, give his daughter away. The bride was beautiful in her mother's gown. The dress fit like it was made for Karla. Miriam's cleaner went out of his way to have the dress cleaned and pressed in time for the wedding. Willow was certain she paid handsomely for that to happen. The dress was old fashioned and modest. Beautiful. The bride even more so. Her long dark hair was piled on top of her head with tiny braids and little curls with pearls throughout. Willow looked twice. Her hair even sparkled. She whispered, "I bet she's been sitting in a stylist's chair since early this morning." She grimaced. Between the itching and the tightening her skirt was seriously making her uncomfortable.

After the lovely ceremony, Willow wandered around mingling with the guests. A few people whispered about Miriam's improved state of being. She had been depressed. Who wouldn't be? She was given a death sentence and her only daughter was a suspect in a murder. While the death sentence still loomed, the daughter situation had improved drastically. The girl was married to the boy her mother had picked out for her so long ago. John New Moon certainly seemed to be a mother-in-law's dream for a son-in-law.

Willow smiled. Of course, he didn't hold a candle to Marshall. She glanced at the couple as they refilled platters.

Embry passed by and peeked at Willow's plate. "What happened to going Vegan?"

Willow looked at the sausage filled mushroom caps on her plate. "That wasn't working too well. I've joined weight watchers. I'm counting points now. I had a ton of vegetables and fruit so I'm able to eat a few appetizers that have a higher point count. It's called eating in moderation."

Embry replied, "Mom, you're gonna have to pick something and stick with it. Nothing will work otherwise."

"I know. I'm just getting a feel for my options. I'm sure one will work out."

Embry raised her eyebrows. "Sometimes I feel like the mother." She kissed Willow's cheek. "Thanks for getting us this job. We're putting everything we can toward the wedding."

"Honey, I told you I have money saved up. Don't worry about it."

"Mom, we don't want to saddle you with the whole bill. We want to help. I've got to get back to work. We'll talk about this later."

Willow watched her responsible, grown-up daughter get back to work. She couldn't believe her baby was getting married.

Steve whispered behind her. "What are you so smiley about?"

She turned. "Just happy. Watching the kids work together. They make a great team."

"That they do."

Willow dropped her napkin and bent over to pick it up when she heard a pop and felt her skirt drop to her ankles. The gasp behind her was loud enough that she was certain she was the cause. Her face was flaming by the time she reached for her skirt and pulled it up around her waist, holding on to the thing for dear life. The pink button that used to hold her skirt in place was in a glass of champagne held by none other than the mother of the bride, Miriam Mitchell. Everyone went silent.

Miriam, not missing a beat, took the button out of her glass and held it up. "Lose something, dear?" Laughter erupted all around.

Willow whispered to Steve. "If you laugh there will be more than one dead body to investigate this week."

Steve's laughter was squelched by teeth clamped on his tongue and by the instinct to live.

A little while later, after the guests were gone and most of the mess was cleaned up, a downtrodden Stan approached Willow and Steve. "Can I talk to you down at the station?"

Steve agreed.

Stan kissed his wife goodbye then followed Steve and Willow, in her safety pin held skirt, to the police station.

Willow stared at Stan through the visor mirror. "What do you think this is all about?"

Steve shook his head. "I have no idea, but I don't think I'm going to like it."

Willow watched from the observation room as Stan confessed to Flynn's murder. She couldn't believe what she was hearing. There was no way that gentle man murdered Flynn, yet, that was exactly what he was saying. She prayed Molly would survive her brother's indiscretion.

"I could not stand by and allow that man to hurt my daughter. I saw red. I followed them to the café. I watched as he smacked her around. She threw the ring then I went in and killed him. It wasn't Daisy. I held him under the water until he went limp."

Willow crinkled her brow. "That isn't right. He's leaving out a lot of details. Like what happened to Daisy's liaison with Flynn after Karla left? What is he doing?" She asked herself.

When Steve took Stan to a cell Willow could not hide her surprise. "He didn't kill Flynn."

"I know it. But he's insisting he did. What am I supposed to do?"

"Send him home. His poor wife is probably freaking out. If Molly knows, she is too."

"He's protecting someone. I'm guessing his daughter. We're gonna need to play this one close to our chest. I don't want to spook anyone.

We want everyone to let down their guards so we can figure out what is happening here."

Willow shook her head. "I don't like it. Not one bit. That woman has terminal cancer. What are we doing to her health?"

"Trust me. This won't last long. Let's let Daisy out. Rumors will spread like wild fire. We'll know the truth soon, very soon."

***

When Willow arrived home, Molly was waiting outside the front door.

"Molly, I would think you'd be home with your feet propped up by now. What brings you out here?" Willow unlocked the door and invited her in, hoping she hadn't heard yet about her brother confessing to the murder.

"I can't stand it anymore, Willow. It's killing me inside."

"What are you talking about?"

"I had a camera installed in the dining room of the restaurant. All these kids keep getting into my café at night and I had some stuff go missing."

"You what?"

"I know. At first I forgot all about it. I've never had a camera system before and it's been a year ago now since I had it put in. It records on a loop. Things were going well and I just didn't think of it." She looked up at Willow. "Until the morning after our double date. The door was unlocked and I immediately went to the camera and that's when I saw it. I saw the whole thing."

Molly was crying in earnest while Willow called Steve.

Steve met Willow and Molly at the café to collect the tape from Molly's security system then sent a relieved Molly home to get some rest. She'd been worrying so much she was unable to go to sleep at night. Steve promised her everything would work out.

Steve walked Willow to her truck. "Why didn't she tell us about this immediately? This would have saved a lot of people a lot of stress, me included."

"I know. She really did forget about it. Out of sight out of mind, ya know?"

"I should charge her with obstruction."

"Steve, you know she didn't mean to. She's been stressing out about everything and she wasn't sure how to tell us. She feels terrible. Especially after what she saw."

"I know she did. And I know she didn't do it on purpose." He looked at his watch. "You told Molly not to say a word to anyone, right?"

"Yep. She promised. Mum's the word."

"OK. Then let's get some rest and I'll call everyone and set up the meeting for tomorrow after lunch. We'll meet at the café, the scene of the crime." He hugged her. "When all this is finished, you and me are going to collapse in front of the television and just hang out together. I feel like I haven't spent any quality time with you." He kissed her then opened her car door for her. "I'll see you tomorrow."

Chapter 16

Willow and Molly prepared lunch for everyone who was attending their meeting. Sandwiches and salads were being offered. The guests entered one by one. The first to arrive was Mrs. Mitchell. Willow was concerned with the toll the whole ordeal was having on her and rightly so. Mrs. Mitchell looked terribly pale. So much so, Willow rushed to her side to help her in.

"Mrs. Mitchell, what's wrong?"

"Please dear, call me Miriam. The doctor said at the most I have six months left. I think it's going to be much sooner. I notice everyday I'm a little weaker. The wedding about did me in. It was good though. I feel much better leaving this world knowing my little girl is going to be taken care of."

"Mrs....I mean, Miriam, can I get you something to eat or drink? We have a nice lunch prepared."

"No dear, I'm not very hungry. Maybe a nice cup of hot tea? Can you do that? I just can't seem to get warm enough." She pulled her sweater tighter around her and shivered.

"Of course. I'll be right back." Willow got Mrs. Mitchell settled then went off in search of hot water and a tea bag. She was returning with the tray when Trevor and Daisy Fisher walked in.

"What's this all about? Why are we being summoned?"

Willow, playing the part of the hostess, smiled and said, "We just want to talk with everyone. Why don't you make yourselves a plate while we wait for the others to arrive? I'm going to take this hot tea to Mrs. Mitchell. Let me know if I can get you anything."

Next to arrive were the newlyweds. Willow wished they didn't have to come back but it was necessary. Steve wanted everyone involved together for the arrest.

She shouldn't have worried. They were newlyweds. They weren't concerned about where they were, as long as they were together. Both John and Karla were all smiles. "Hey, we're here." He called out as he playfully pulled his young bride into an embrace.

Willow smiled back. "I bet you two are hungry. Come get a sandwich and some salad. There's chips too. Help yourself to some ice tea or lemonade." She pointed toward the spread. She and Molly did a pretty good job considering the whole meeting was called the evening before.

The last to arrive was Steve with Stan in tow. Stan was still handcuffed. When he entered the café, everyone stopped chatting and eating, and remembered what they were doing there. Something was going on. This meeting wasn't called for the fun of it.

Willow still hated what they were doing to Miriam. She wasn't strong enough and hearing her audible gasp at her husband in handcuffs sent Willow running to her side. "Miriam, are you OK?"

She gasped for air. "No, I'm not OK. My husband..." She paused, her eyes filling with tears.

Karla went to her mother's side, finally acting the concerned daughter. "Mom. What can I do?"

Miriam tried to buck up but her ailment wasn't allowing it. "I'll never understand how one can grow so weak so fast." She took a few deep breaths. "Karla, make your father a plate. He doesn't need to be on display for everyone to watch. You know what he likes."

Karla obeyed her mother and took her father a plate and a glass of ice tea. Steve removed his handcuffs so he could eat.

While Stan was eating, Steve approached Willow. "Looks like our plan is working."

Willow nodded. "This is harder than I thought it would be."

"I know. It's almost over. Be strong."

After lunch Steve rolled out a television and a DVD player. He hit play and watched the faces of those seated around him.

Karla gasped when Flynn dropped her to the floor with a swift punch from his fist. She watched the ring she flung at him drop in the water. He went for the ring first, giving her time to get out of the restaurant before he could hit her again.

They all watched Flynn pace the floor then make a telephone call. A little bit later Daisy entered. As Daisy watched her part in the events unfolding on screen, she had the good graces to blush.

Steve fast forwarded through much of what happened next. No point in embarrassing the girl more than she already was. The important fact was Flynn was very much alive when she left the café.

Different sounds came forth from every person watching the television when the next person walked into the camera's viewing area. Mrs. Mitchell fainted. Mr. Mitchell screamed, "No." Karla placed her hand over mouth and started sobbing.

Everyone else sat in stunned silence as they watched Miriam, Karla's mother, murder Flynn Allen.

Chapter 17

The ambulance rushed Miriam Mitchell to the hospital. The stress of her husband taking the blame then being found out put her over the edge. She wasn't going to be much longer for this world.

After the hospital got her comfortable, Steve and Willow found themselves sitting by her bedside. She wanted to confess what she'd done—and why—before the drugs made her loopy.

Her voice was so soft, both Willow and Steve had to edge as close as they possibly could to the bed. She smiled. "First, I want you to know I'm not sorry for what I did. I would do it all over again if I had to."

Willow completely understood. Steve thought he did.

"I noticed the bruises shortly after she came home. I asked her about them but she would always make up some sort of excuse. I knew I wouldn't be around to pick up the pieces, to hold my little girl any more. When he stormed out I knew she would follow him and he would hit her again. If she kept seeing him he would eventually kill her. I knew it. And I wouldn't be here to talk reason to her, to help her see how wrong he was for her. I followed her straight to the café. I watched him hit my little girl." She looked up at Willow and Steve, dark rings under her eyes. "You saw him. He punched her in the face and put her on the floor. I saw him do that and I went crazy. I knew in my state I'd be no match for him physically so I drove home and got our ranch's cattle prod then I went back to the café.

"When I returned, Daisy was already with him. I was flabbergasted. I thought Daisy was Karla's friend. I had no idea she was more Flynn's friend than Karla's. I waited for her to go then I went into the café and confronted him. He laughed at me. He told me my daughter was a piece of garbage and he'd only used her to get away from the people coming for him. Once he got out of their reach he'd discard her like he did the rest of his garbage. He was proud of himself. I couldn't believe it. He laughed at me. I pulled out the cattle prod and I shocked him."

She asked for a drink of water then continued. "Even in a incapacitated position, unable to move, he still laughed at me. His eyes still mocked me. He would never leave her alone.

I knew it. A mother knows these things. So, I shocked him again. This time he wasn't smiling. I think that's when he realized I had the upper hand, even in my state of health. I gathered up every bit of energy I had left and I positioned his head over the water and I sat on his back until he was still." She looked for judgement from both Steve and Willow and found sadness, but not judgement. "Then I left."

Mr. Mitchell had been standing at the door, tears silently dripping as he listened.

Steve turned toward him. "You were trying to protect your wife?"

"No. I didn't know she followed Karla. We had an emergency at work I needed to go deal with. I thought Karla did it. When I got home I noticed the cattle prod wasn't hanging in the garage. I thought it was weird but didn't think about it again until the next day when I heard Flynn was dead. I thought my daughter finally had enough of his torment."

He hung his head. "I'm sorry I didn't mention that earlier. I just…" He closed his eyes and took a deep breath. "…I wasn't even sure the cattle prod was connected. It was a theory, that was all. She has her whole life in front of her and I didn't want her suffering for protecting herself."

Miriam's eyes would fall then open again a few seconds later. The nurse came in and checked her vitals. She smiled then exited the room.

Karla and John were in the hallway. Steve looked to Willow and nodded toward the door.

Miriam opened her eyes and pleaded with Willow. "Please don't hate me. I didn't know what else to do. I couldn't leave this earth without knowing she was going to be OK."

Willow gently held her hand. "I don't know if I would have done what you did. I can't say. I've never been in that position. But, I will say there is nothing I wouldn't do to protect my daughter. I would gladly give my life for her. I'm not judging you. And I certainly don't hate you. I can even understand the helplessness you felt." She smiled. "Your daughter and son-in-law want to spend some time with you." Willow let go of her hand and followed Steve out of the room.

Neither one said anything as they walked the hospital corridor. Steve held the truck door open for her and quietly drove the distance to the café, where Willow had left her Jeep.

He parked and neither one moved. Willow's tears were marking her sweatshirt. Steve pulled her close. "Mind if I come over for a while?"

She nodded and snuggled into him.

Chapter 18

Willow pulled the turkey out of the oven and studied it. *A masterpiece.* She basted the bird and put it back in the oven. The stuffing peeking out from the cavity smelled good enough to eat right then. Her grandmother's fine china dressed the table. Table service for eight. The delicate dishes reminded Willow of the times she visited as a young girl. Her grandmother would serve dinner on them simply because Willow was obsessed with them. *Some things never change.*

The potatoes were cubed and in the pot, ready to boil. The sweet potato soufflé was prepared. The Brussel sprouts cleaned. The rolls baked. Everything looked perfect.

Clover refused to move from the oven. "The bird is dead, Clover. It's not a threat." The dog looked to her then back at the oven. "OK, have it your way." She shook her head then headed for the bedroom.

Her diet had been progressing well and she'd lost enough weight to wear the skirt she'd worn for the wedding—bonus, it buttoned without wrapping herself in a bunch of plastic wrap. Not wanting a repeat, she wore the long flowy blouse she'd picked out previously, just in case. She twirled and smiled. Every day was one step closer to a better, healthier Willow.

She put on a little lip gloss and a little mascara, brushed her auburn hair, and put on her diamond stud earrings. She glanced at herself in the mirror and smiled.

The doorbell rang. Steve, looking more handsome than ever stood at the threshold with a gorgeous bouquet of fall flowers. He kissed her then handed her the flowers. "For you." He stepped back. "You look ravishing. Are you sure we have to have guests over?"

She wiggled her eyebrows then turned for the kitchen while he went back to his truck. He'd agreed to pick up soda and tea.

A few minutes later Marshall and Embry pulled in. Steve pulled Willow close. "I better get a good hug in before everyone comes in. Who knows how long they all plan on staying."

"Behave yourself!"

The kids, Willow still thought of her daughter as her kid even though she was 23 years old, came in and looked suspiciously at their guilty faces. Embry spoke up. "I don't even want to know."

Willow laughed.

"Where do you want the cranberry relish and charcuterie?"

"Cranberry relish in the fridge, charcuterie on the appetizer table in the living room."

Marshall helped Embry get the meat and cheese board laid out for guests while Steve helped Willow in the kitchen.

The doorbell rang again. "Embry, would you get that?" Willow had her hands full.

"Sure, Mom."

Molly and Trevor entered next with Molly's famous pies. She was providing pumpkin, apple, and pecan pies. Willow took one whiff and was thankful carb cycling offered one free day a week. "These look fantastic. I have a small table set up in the corner of the dining room for dessert. Why don't you put them there? Or should they be refrigerated?"

"Let's put the pumpkin in the refrigerator, the pecan and apple should be fine sitting out."

Trevor held up the ice cream and whipping cream—real whipped cream, not the stuff in a tub. Willow took them and put them away. "Maybe we should skip ahead to dessert."

Molly pulled Willow aside. "Stan's coming. I told him not to worry about bringing anything. He almost didn't come. These last few weeks have been hard on him, being his first

Thanksgiving without Miriam. They were married for almost thirty years. Took them five years before she got pregnant with Karla. She was their miracle baby."

Willow sighed. "Did John and Karla go to his parents today?"

Molly shook her head. "No, he surprised her with a cruise. Looks like she's getting her Caribbean honeymoon after all."

"Good. I'm glad they got away. With the murder, the last-minute wedding, and their short honeymoon interrupted, they deserve to spend some quality time together. They have a lot to catch up on."

"The funeral was sad. The murder cast a dark pall and those who attended were more somber than usual. It broke my heart that some people didn't bother coming. She was obviously not thinking clearly. I felt really bad for Stan and Karla." Willow placed her hand on Molly's arm. "For you too, of course."

"No worries, dear. I know exactly what you mean. She had tumors growing throughout her body, including a large brain tumor. She couldn't have been in her right mind. She never would have done what she had done if she hadn't had been sick." She took a sip of her tea. "I have to believe that. She's in heaven now, singing with the angels."

Willow smiled and squeezed Molly's hand.

The doorbell rang once again. Willow answered. "Janie." She hugged her friend close. "I'm so glad you could come."

"Where else was I going to go?" She smiled. "And where else would I rather be?"

She held up her offerings for the appetizer table. "Where do these go?"

Willow pointed to the table with the charcuterie. "Right there. Need anything?"

"Nope. I've it covered." Willow went to shut the door and noticed Stan standing against his truck. She pulled on her sweater and went outside.

"Hey, you coming in?"

"I haven't decided."

His sadness nearly broke her heart. "You know you're among friends here."

He smiled, thankful for her kindness. "I know. I miss my wife."

"I've never lost a spouse, but I have lost both my parents and my grandparents. I'll be honest. The pain never goes away. I go longer in-between thinking about my pain, but it's always there, just waiting for that small reminder. Your pain is so very new. Don't let anyone tell you what you can and can't feel. I would love for you to come in, even if only for a little while."

She held out her hand and he took it. Together they walked the distance to her front door. "Hey everyone, Stan made it."

She smiled and left him in Steve's capable hands.

"Marshall, would you add another log to the fire please?"

"I'd love to, Mom."

She looked up in surprise with a great big grin on her face.

A little while later, with music playing softly in the background, eight people sat around the Thanksgiving table laden with food, surrounded by friends, and thankful for their blessings.

Steve said grace, "Lord, we thank you for your gifts of family and friends. We thank you for another blessed year. I pray we always remember from where every good gift comes. And we thank you for this wonderful meal you have provided for us. Bless those around this table, and loves ones who cannot be with us today, with your love and mercy. Amen."

Willow's Pumpkin Roll

- 3 eggs, separated
- 1 cup sugar, divided in half
- 2/3 cup pumpkin
- ¾ cup flour
- 1 Tsp. baking soda
- ½ Tsp. cinnamon
- ¼ Tsp. salt

Frosting:
- 8 oz cream cheese, softened
- 2 Tbsp. butter
- 1 ½ cup powdered sugar
- ½ Tsp. vanilla

Preheat oven to 375 degrees F.

Line jelly roll pan with parchment paper and grease paper. (very important step)

Beat egg yolks until thick. Gradually add ½ cup sugar and pumpkin. Beat until most of sugar dissolves.

Whip egg whites until soft peaks form. Fold into pumpkin mixture. Sift dry ingredients and fold into pumpkin mixture.

Pour onto prepared jelly roll pan and spread evenly with a small spatula. Tap pan on counter to help distribute batter for an even cake.

Bake 13-15 minutes.

Remove cake and immediately turn cake onto a clean, fragrance free tea towel. Remove parchment paper. Roll tightly to cool. Do not allow cake to cool before rolling. The odds of cracking will be much higher if you do.

Let cake cool completely.

Beat cream cheese, butter, powdered sugar, and vanilla.

Unroll cake and spread frosting evenly leaving about ½ inch on all sides. The frosting will spread when the cake is re-rolled. Once cake is frosted, roll cake back up.

Wrap tightly in plastic wrap then a layer of aluminum foil. Refrigerate or freeze cake roll. Slicing is easier if you freeze it.

Sprinkle with a dusting of powdered sugar before serving.

Willow's Apple Pie

- 6 large apples, mixed variety
- ½ cup sugar
- ½ cup dark brown sugar-firmly packed
- 2 Tbsp. flour
- ½ Tsp. nutmeg
- ¼ Tsp. cinnamon
- 2 Tbsp. butter

Prepare crust (see next recipe) Preheat oven to 375 degrees F. Peel, core, and thinly slice apples. Transfer to bowl. In a separate bowl combine sugars, flour, and spices. Sprinkle 1/3 of sugar mixture into the bottom of pastry lined pie pan. Toss apples with ½ of remaining sugar mixture. Mound apples in pan. Sprinkle with remaining sugar. Dot with butter. Fold top crust under edges of bottom crust. Pinch to seal. Vent top crust. Beat 1 egg white. Brush on top crust. Bake 50-60 minutes.

Note: If edge of crust starts to darken, cover edges with aluminum foil.

Willow's Pie Crust

From Lilly's great, great, grandmother

- 4 cups flour
- 1 Tbsp. sugar
- 2 Tsp. salt
- 1 ½ cups shortening
- 1 egg
- 1 Tbsp. vinegar
- ½ cup water

Mix flour, sugar, and salt in bowl. Cut in shortening till crumbs are size of peas. Beat egg, vinegar, and water. Sprinkle over flower mixture and mix well with a fork.

Flour surface and rolling pin. Roll out dough.

Makes 2 double crusts.

Willow's German Apple Cake

- 2 large eggs
- 1 cup salad oil
- 2 cups sugar
- 1 Tsp. vanilla
- 2 cups flour
- 3 Tsp. cinnamon
- 1 Tsp. baking soda
- ½ Tsp. salt
- 4 cups sliced apples, peeled
- ½ cup chopped walnuts

Preheat oven to 350 degrees, F.

Beat eggs and salad oil until light and fluffy. Add sugar, vanilla, flour, cinnamon, baking soda, and salt. (batter will be heavy.) Add apples and nuts. Turn into a greased 9 x 13 pan. Bake for 45-60 minutes (until toothpick comes out clean).

Frosting:

8 ounces cream cheese, softened
3 Tbsp. butter, softened
1 Tsp. vanilla
2 cups powdered sugar

Mix until smooth and spread on cooled cake.

Please enjoy this excerpt from 'The Chocolate Kiss of Death', Book 6 of the Willow Crier Cozy Mystery Series

Willow looked at herself in the full-length mirror. She turned in a circle, admiring the svelte person staring back. She started carb cycling and for her, it was working. She liked every kind of food and one day a week she got a free day. There were weeks she lived for those free days but she could stay strong in-between, most of the time.

She walked around the room. The caterers did a lovely job. They were still finishing up the last-minute touches. The guests would be arriving in a couple of hours. She had wanted a few minutes alone with her thoughts. The photo albums of the kids were on the gift table. She glanced through Embry's—stopping on photographs that brought strong memories. Some made her smile, some gave her pause. Her newborn picture. She didn't cry. She looked around curious and nosy—traits that remained all through her life and would probably carry her through to the end.

Her preschool picture with her frog backpack. That was the first time of many she made Willow cry. She didn't want Willow walking her into school. What four-year-old does that? She wanted to walk in by herself without her mother. Willow shook her head. Independence, sometimes referred to as stubbornness, also stuck to her like glue.

Willow flipped through the school years landing on her high school graduation. The little girl grew up to be a beautiful young woman. Willow couldn't be more proud of her. She started college then decided to wait and figure out what she wanted to do with her life. She decided, and it had nothing to do with a college education. She was going to be a wife and a mother. Willow smiled. She remembered her daughter's description of the house she would live in—in the country, across from Willow's, with a creek and a bridge separating them so she could bring her children over whenever she needed a babysitter. Willow tried to remind Embry of that promise to no avail. Her daughter had grown up and her dreams had grown too.

Willow stopped at her engagement picture. Marshall's face glowed. The love he had for her daughter would last a lifetime. She thought about her own mistakes and thanked God her daughter hadn't made the same. Sure, she'd experience pain, but she would also know true love and happiness.

The doorbell interrupted Willow's walk through time. She glanced at her watch. Whoever it is, was way too early. She let everyone know, even Steve, she wanted a little time by herself before anyone arrived. Otherwise her mascara would be sure to run. She had no plans to put her make up on until the last minute—perhaps she would spend her tears by then. Clover growled at the door, waiting to protect Willow from danger.

She opened the door and met her own past face to face then slammed it. The doorbell rang again. She re-opened it. "What do you want?"

"Nice welcome for a guy you haven't seen in, what, over 20 years?"

"I could stand another 20 if you don't mind. You can leave now." She tried to close the door but he inserted his foot before it closed. Too bad she didn't have her gun on her. She could claim intruder and shoot the jerk.

The dog barked, her hair standing on end.

"Again I ask, what do you want?"

He glanced nervously at the dog. *Good*, she thought, *he should be afraid, very afraid.*

"I want to talk. Is that so much to ask? Our daughter is engaged and going to be married. I thought a civil conversation might be in order."

"How do you know she's engaged?"

His face contorted into a superior, know it all look she remembered only too well. "She told me. How do you think?"

He was full of himself. And proud. Why she had no idea. "We both know you're not here because of Embry. You've never been here for her. What do you really want?"

He reached out and caressed her cheek before she realized what he was doing. "I think we should give it another go. You know, for Embry's sake."

"Give what a go? You can't mean—a relationship?" Borrowing a phrase from her daughter she added, "Are you freaking kidding me?" She paused. "Oh, I get it. You heard I've inherited money. I noticed you didn't show up on my doorstep when you could have been taken to court for child support. Just so you know, I can still take you to court. Let's see…18 years of child support…you probably owe about a half a mil with interest? Give or take?"

His cockiness disappeared. "Hey. I'm just here because Embry asked me to come. That's it. I don't want anything from you."

"The party doesn't start until 6. Come back then." She ushered him out the door then picked up the phone. No answer. Willow slammed the phone, well, she slammed the phone in her head. She missed house phones that had a nice base you could actually slam the receiver into. iPhones were kind of hard to slam. You could only push the little button so hard without jamming your finger. She sure missed the good ole days. Sometimes.

She paced back and forth. Paced might be too tempered, stomped was more like it. Clover found a corner and covered her head with her paws.

Embry wasn't answering her phone. Willow could only leave so many voicemails and still be considered sane. Although she supposed it didn't really matter if her daughter considered her to be sane. At least until she tried to have her committed to gain control of her assets. Not that Embry would ever do such a thing. At least Willow hoped she wouldn't.

She punched in Steve's number. She had to talk to someone. He answered on the first ring and she immediately erupted, telling him

[153]

everything that happened. And when she finished, she busted out in tears. The only thing she heard on the other end of the line was, "I'll be right over."

A few minutes later she was crying on his shoulder. "I told you he wasn't an issue. Now he's back." She sniffled. "I tried to call Embry. She isn't answering. The man hasn't paid a single dime in child support, he's never been there for her, why would she call him?"

Steve ran his hand over her hair. "He's her dad. This is a once in a lifetime moment for her. Every child holds out that somehow, someway, even when all the evidence points elsewhere, the absent parent will whisk into their lives and suddenly become everything they have missed out on over the years. Even grown kids hope. Even Embry wants a dad."

"How did you get to be so smart on parenting?" What she really wanted to say was *until you have kids stuff it* but she didn't go there.

"Remember, I work at the shelter every week. I still volunteer and work with kids who are being raised without one, and sometimes two parents. Every single one of them dream they'll be reunited someday. Embry isn't the exception."

"I know she said she was going to call him but I thought she might have backed out—that she wouldn't go through with it. And why wouldn't she tell me? I have 50 people coming over in less than an hour and I'm a mess. I could have been better prepared."

"Honey, she did try to tell you. You wouldn't listen."

Willow's eyebrows furrowed.

"I'm not trying to be mean. I'm just reminding you, your daughter did tell you."

Willow took a few deep breaths and dabbed her eyes with a tissue. "You're right. I'm sorry. I need to grow up."

"I imagine it's difficult seeing your little girl grow up and need someone other than you. You have nothing to be sorry for." He let her cry on his shoulder a little while longer then gently reminded her the guest would be arriving shortly.

She nodded. The caterers were sticking close to the kitchen while she cried. She went to the bedroom to freshen up and put some make-up on while Steve let the caterers know they had free reign once again.

Embry and Marshall were the first to arrive. Willow's red swollen eyes alerted Embry to her father's arrival.

"I take it dad showed up."

Willow nodded.

"Did you send him away?"

[155]

Willow shook her head.

Embry looked to Steve for some verbal information.

Steve smiled slightly. "He'll be back at six."

Embry widened her eyes. "So, Mom, you're letting him come."

Willow swallowed the frog in her throat. "If it means that much to you, then yes." She dabbed her eyes. "I don't want to start crying again so let's just change the subject. Okay?"

Embry nodded. She fully empathized with her mother. She hated for anyone to see her cry too.

Willow bit her lip and went to the kitchen. "Do you need any help?"

She was shooed out of the kitchen so she checked the fire. Steve had already added another log. It was crackling just fine.

She turned from the fireplace and went in search of something to do, anything to do. This night was supposed to be perfect. Everyone she knew was coming to celebrate Embry's engagement. She needed to pull herself together. *Why did I think he wouldn't come? Why didn't I prepare myself for the worst?* She ducked into her bedroom to take a few deep breaths. *Come on, Willow. You can do this. You're made of stronger stuff than this!*

She had no idea why but lately she'd been more emotional. She was a straight shooter. A woman who saw the logic in things and pretty much called it as she saw it. The girls in college would cry over commercials and Willow wondered what was wrong with them. Now, it was her turn. Especially if the commercial had to do with kids growing up and leaving.

Willow decided to talk to her doctor. Maybe she was peri-menopausal. *There must be some reason I'm acting like this!*

The doorbell rang and she took a deep breath. *I shouldn't have any more time to be morose.* Her guests would keep her busy.

As the evening spent, Willow found herself loosening up and laughing. Every time the doorbell rang, she would jump a little but each time, the person on the other side was a friend of hers or Embry and Mitchells. She had to admit, she finally started to worry a little, especially when she caught sight of the frown lines on her daughter's face.

Guests were milling around, eating hors d'oevres, and chatting with the young couple about their wedding plans. Willow finally figured Alex wasn't coming. He'd disappointed her daughter once again. Perhaps she would learn her lesson. Willow learned long ago the man was not to be trusted. She was about to pull Embry aside when the doorbell rang.

Willow answered the door. Alex stood on the other side. He tried to straighten his windblown hair and make himself presentable before facing his grown daughter. Without thinking, Willow reached out to wipe some chocolate from the corner of his mouth.

He took a quick step backwards. "What are you doing?"

"You have a little something…" She pointed.

He touched the side of his face. "Here?"

She shook her head. "No, down, by the corner of your mouth."

His eyes lit up. "You can kiss it off. Nothing more intimate than a little chocolate kiss between lovers."

A deep voice behind her said, "Lovers?"

Alex swept by her, smiled, and shook Steve's hand. "Hi, I'm Alex. Willow's ex."

"I'm Steve. Willow's current."

Willow looked at both men. "Hello, I'm right here."

Alex turned back to her and lowered his voice to a loud whisper, making sure Steve heard every word. "No worries, I won't forget about you that easily."

Willow rolled her eyes and shook her head as she walked away, motioning toward Embry as she went. Steve stood a good six inches taller than Alex so he crossed his arms and stared the man down as he traipsed after Embry.

He watched the young woman hug her dad. The room wasn't large enough to hide from her excitement.

"You made it!" Embry giggled.

Steve groaned then caught up with Willow.

A Yankee's Guide to Southern Phrases

Bless Your Heart: The most back handed kind words spoken in the south. Means, while you're sweet, you're also stupid, you don't quite get it and I feel sorry for you.

Fixin to: About to do something, almost ready, thinking about doing something.

Nervous as a long tail cat in a room full of rockin' chairs: Nervous to the point of being jumpy.

Reckon: So suppose or believe something is true.

Yankee: Anyone originating north of the Mason Dixon line.

Redneck: Polite, blue collar individual who loves hunting, country music, and blue jeans. Add alcohol and anything can happen.

Y'all: You guys

All y'all: More than five people

I could eat the north end of a south-bound polecat: Starving!

Lil' Dogie: A motherless calf, a calf separated from its cow.

Hankering: Craving something
Fair to middlin': Doing okay
Three sheets to the wind: Drunker than a skunk
Passel: A whole bunch
Hold your horses: Be patient
Grinning like a possum eating a sweet potato: Happy as can be
He's a snake in the grass: Mean as all get out
Gussied Up: Dressed fancy

Author Bio

Lilly York? How about Lilly Belle; a mis-plant northerner, living in a southern world. Southern charm is lost among late nights with a two year old granddaughter, heat flashes competing with hell, copious re-runs of Murder She Wrote with Jessica Fletcher catching the bad guy, and a vivid imagination keeping insanity at bay.

In both humor and mystery, Lilly draws inspiration from terrible twos, a 24 year old daughter who questions her sanity, a son who constantly spews bad puns, and a husband who has selective hearing. Though, that's perfectly alright with her, because what can you love more than a good laugh and a family so dysfunctional they almost seem functional?

Make sure you visit her at:

LillyYork.com